CW00418257

SEMPER FI

And Other Short Stories

Thomas M. Woodland

Also Available

The Man Who Isn't There

Contents

Foreword

Well, here we are again.

First off, I need to apologise for things said in the introduction of my previous collection of short stories. Honestly, I look back at that now and cringe. "Writing is man's greatest gift", who the hell did I think I was? Not some nineteen-year-old kid who's self-publishing his first work, that's for certain. Guess there's a reason I'm still saved as "Pretentious Prick" in my sister's phone (you were right all along, Soph - but don't let it go to your head). And honestly, that bit about encouraging young writers to enter short story competitions? That might sound all right coming from Anthony Horowitz or John Grisham, or any other writer who's actually earned some acclaim. But from a first-time writer with barely any life experience? Christ, does it sound patronising and big-headed. And why, why on earth, did I decide to fire shots at J.K. Rowling, then attempt to immediately placate the fans I'd just offended? Like, come on past me, if you're gonna take a stance like that, at least stick to it. So, yeah. I'm sorry for that extremely ill-advised foreword. I promise that will not happen again.

So, to this collection. There are, I'm afraid, still some elements of pretentiousness in these stories, particularly in the ones from when I was still at school. Thankfully, the older, wiser me of 2023 can recognise those elements, and I do call myself out on them in my author's comments on each story. Speaking of, I'm trying to be a little more candid to the faults in these stories this time. Last time, I think I was going all out to try and impress people, over explaining and pontificating on every little detail of the stories. Well, that's not the goal of this collection. This one, with stories that span from 2016 all the way to 2020, maps out my journey as a writer over recent years. And what a set of years they've been. Even in the four years since I published *The Man Who Isn't There*, things have changed drastically. I've gained a degree and started a job. I've been through a major relationship and breakup. The world has been through a pandemic (let's be honest, is kinda still going through it). And, most relevantly, I've started, and finished, a full novel. In short, both my writing and I have matured a lot, and I hope you can see that over the course of this collection.

I'll drop a general content warning here. There are some things in some of these stories that are really not pleasant. A couple of them (I'll provide warnings at the beginning of each) feature some quite graphic and gruesome violence that some people may not want to read about. Please feel free to skip those stories if you're worried they will upset you. Secondly, there are a couple of stories in this collection that touch on or deal with the theme of mental illness. I'll be the first to admit, I am far from an expert in this subject. I know bits and pieces, here and there, but nothing in depth. The depictions I present here almost certainly do not ring true to genuine mental illness, and they should not be taken as accurate representations. They were just what made the most sense to the stories that I was trying to tell. If I cause anyone any offense through the depictions in those stories, I am truly sorry. Please do feel free to reach out and educate me on these matters; I'm always keen to learn more.

I think that's about all I wanted to say in this prelude. Thank you for buying my book, particularly if you also bought *The Man Who Isn't There* (and doubly so if you're someone I don't know personally!).

Putting it together has been something of task, particularly since I decided before I started that I wasn't going to edit any of the stories (beyond correcting any typographical errors – something that, at time of writing, I still need to do for the last collection). I wanted this to be a true representation of how my writing has changed over time, and to edit any of the content of these stories would taint that representation. It's like a nudist beach; the good, the bad, and the ugly – you're going to see it all.

And on that note, I'll end this ramble. I hope you enjoy the stories.

Thomas M. Woodland

Tick Tock Goes the Croc

The two blades, one slender and elegant, one short and stubby, flashed silver in the moonlight atop the cliffs. Anyone watching, on that fateful night, might have seen two figures engaging in a strange kind of dance, silhouetted against the great white moon. One was tall, well built, a long greatcoat swishing around his ankles. Long, elegant mustachios twirled from above his lips, and a wide brimmed hat sat on his head, a long feather pluming from the brim. His sturdy leather boots darted over the ground as he deftly leapt forward and backward, his arm twisting and turning like a snake with every thrust of his rapier.

The other figure was smaller, more slender and seemingly even more agile than his opponent. His feet hardly seemed to be touching the ground at all as he skipped around his enemy, jabbing and slashing with the dagger, nimbly avoiding every attack. He turned an elegant cartwheel to avoid a thrust, somehow not losing his peaked hat, his own feather tickling the grass as he spun. A golden belt buckle twinkled at his waist as he regained his footing, still facing the other figure. A small ball of light, pure white, hovered above his shoulder, scattering silver dust as it moved.

The larger silhouette lunged forward again, snarling.

"You think you can beat me boy?" he asked, swiping at his opponent's face. "I've taught you everything you know. I took you in, and this is how you repay me?"

"You took me in because you needed me," the boy retorted, parrying the attack with the flat of his blade.

"I needed you?" the man roared. "You were a lonely, scared boy who'd run away from home! You had nothing, and no one! I fed you, clothed you, taught you to fight! That dagger is mine, that tunic is mine, that belt is mine!"

"You taught me too well, old man," the boy answered. "And you think I'm alone? I've found others, others like me. This island belongs to us now, and you and your crew are hereby being evicted!"

So saying, the boy leapt into the air, and flew, arms outstretched, over the other man's head. The rapier flashed upwards, aiming for the boy's stomach, the tip poised to unzip him from naval to sternum. The boy twisted in the air, swerved around the blade, continued past the man. He banked, turned in the air, and came back, slashing with his dagger as he did so. The dagger that the other man had given him as a present for completing his training.

The other man's rapier fell to the ground. It bounced off a rock and, with the hand still holding it, tumbled off the cliff edge. The man howled, clutching the stump of his wrist, dark liquid dripping from between his fingers. The boy spun once in the air, and planted a foot firmly in the centre of the man's chest, right on the ruffles of his dress shirt. The man wobbled, flailed, and fell backwards, twisting through the air until he hit the water far below. The boy twirled in the air, sheathed his dagger, and flew off into the night.

The man sank beneath the waves, blood pluming from his wrist, pain and shock overriding his brain. He went down, down, almost to the bottom, hanging in the water amongst the wreck of a ship. He opened his eyes, and was amazed to find he could see. An eerie green light was emanating from all around him, penetrating easily through the crystal-clear water. The rocks on the seabed and cliff wall were glowing, like an oil lamp but all-encompassing. The wreck was old, the wood rotting and the hull split on the seabed. The open mouth of the hole yawned at him, a place that none of the green light seemed to reach.

Something glittered on the seabed, a tail of black twisting upwards from its base.

His rapier, his severed hand still attached to the handle, was lying in front of him. The sight of it, with his blood, dark in the water, made him feel sick.

His eyes were stinging from the salt water, and he shut them, knowing that his tears would be lost anyway. When he opened them again, his heart stopped.

There was a dark shape, thick and long, twisting through the water towards him. Through his squinting, stinging eyes, he saw four short, stubbly legs hanging beneath it as it wriggled. A long, muscular tail thrashed suddenly behind it, propelling it forward with a great burst of speed. Its head split open as its jaws gaped, wide enough to swallow him whole.

A crocodile.

The man reacted instinctively, despite his lungs straining and eyes hurting and pain from his recent amputation nearly blinding him. With his remaining left hand, he scrabbled for his sword, shook the severed hand free, and swiped at the animal as it lunged at him. It deftly twisted away, sailing past him just as the boy had on the clifftop. The man flailed in the water, thrashing with his arms and legs to propel himself away from the hideous creature. He struggled blindly through the water, lungs beginning to burn as his air continued to drain away.

The open mouth of the cracked hull swallowed him up as he disappeared into the wreck. Looking back, he watched in horror as the crocodile dipped lower in the water, and closed its jaws around his severed hand. It engulfed it whole, looking up at him even as it disappeared down its gullet. Blurred as his vision was, he could see in the creature's vile yellow eyes that it wasn't satisfied. It had got a taste for him. His hand had been the starter. Now it was time for the main course.

He flailed further into the wreck, passing through the galley and into the sleeping quarters. The crocodile followed him, lazily drifting through the water. It didn't hurry. It knew he was trapped.

And trapped he was.

There was no way out of the crew's quarters. The trapdoor in the ceiling was rotted shut, the wood swollen and warped. He turned back, hoping to get out before the creature reached him, but it was too late. It was hanging there in the doorway, watching him.

His lungs were tearing themselves apart. He was running out of air, slowly bleeding out from a wound inflicted by the boy he had treated like a son, with a perfectly evolved killing machine no more than a few feet away. He weakly held out his sword before him, but it did no good. His strength was failing him, and the weapon fell from his fingers. He closed his eyes. He didn't want to see it happen.

And then he heard it.

A ticking sound, coming from next to him, by one of the bunks.

He opened his eyes, and saw ...

An alarm clock. A mechanical alarm clock, seemingly untouched by the salt water. The man could see the numerals and hands glowing faintly in the darkness as it ticked on.

Without thinking, without even being sure what he was doing, he snatched it up, and hurled it forward as the crocodile, sensing something had changed, lunged forward. The device, chunky and metallic, tumbled through the water in slow motion, and disappeared into the creature's throat.

The jaws, lined with mountain ridges of white teeth, snapped shut. The creature shuddered, choking, convulsing at the foreign object that had been jammed into its oesophagus. It twisted in the water, squirming in pain as it tried to swallow the clock.

New strength filled the man's veins. He snatched up his sword, forced it between the edge of the trapdoor and the wood around it, and levered with all his strength, lungs screaming at him as the last of his supply ran out. The wood creaked, splintered, but held. He levered again, and this time, the planks split, the panel breaking as the rotten planks fell apart. The man surged upwards desperately as the crocodile managed to swallow the clock and hurl itself at him again.

But the trapdoor was too small. The crocodile could get no more than its snout through the narrow opening. The man couldn't hear the crocodile's roar of anger, didn't even know if crocodiles could roar. But he could still hear the ticking of the clock that had saved his life. He dropped the sword, watching it sink back into the depths, and kicked for the surface, watching the last of his air drift past him in precious silver bubbles. He couldn't take it anymore. He had to open his mouth and breathe, even if it was just water that rushed down his throat and into his lungs. He had to do it.

And suddenly, his mouth was wrenched open in a silent scream as his head broke the surface. He greedily sucked in air; sweet, sweet air.

Never before had it felt so good to breathe. For a moment, he lay on his back, tears streaming down his cheeks, looking up at the moon.

And then, he saw the dark shape flash across it in the dark sky, the tiny light still flying alongside them as they whipped through the air.

The man felt hatred begin to boil his blood. A fire ignited within him and he surged forwards in the water, swimming as fast as his remaining limbs would let him, each stroke fuelled by fury. That boy. The boy he had found as a snivelling wreck, the boy he had taken in as part of his crew. The boy who he'd seen fight, shout, drink, and laugh with the rest of them. The boy who'd refused to grow up, but who'd developed so much since he'd taken him in.

That boy had just cut off his hand and left him for dead.

That boy was going to pay. Him, and his damn fairy.

The man reached the shore and pulled himself up onto the beach. It was only now that the thought of blood loss occurred to him. Quickly, he pulled off his belt and wrapped it tightly around his bicep, forcing the steel pin through the leather to make a new hole, taking care not to look at the wound. It was risky; he could end up losing his entire forearm and not just his wrist. But when he weighed that against losing his life, it was an easy choice. After all, he could still take revenge on the boy with only one arm.

The journey back to his ship would normally have taken him no more than half an hour, an easy walk through a thin forest on flat ground. But with blood loss, shock and anger clouding his mind, it wasn't until two hours later that he stumbled up the gangplank. The deck was deserted, the crew asleep.

He tried to call out for his first mate, but the words came out as no more than a croak. His legs gave out beneath him, and he collapsed to the deck. He was half aware of a door opening, of shouts for help, but it all felt disconnected. The last thought to pass through his head was that he was not going to die before that boy had felt his wrath. Then, all was black.

*

Pain.

That was first thing he knew.

Not the sharp, cutting pain of his initial injury, but the dull, agonising ache of something that would not go away.

Slowly, his eyes cracked open. He could see shadows dancing on the wooden ceiling above him, jumping and weaving from the flickering of the candle and the rocking of the boat.

"Ah, uh, Captain. You're awake."

The Irish-tinted voice was that of his bosun, and he sounded afraid. The man sat up, despite his crewman's efforts to push him back down.

"B-b-b-but, Captain, the doctor said you need your rest."

"Take your hands off me," the man snapped. He tried to put his hands down on the shelf next to his bunk in his quarters, but something clunked as he did so. He glanced down, and shrieked.

There was a bloody bandage wrapped around his wrist, the material dotted with dark stains. But the stains were black, not red. A terrible, empty black.

"Ah-h-h-h-h. Yes, C-c-c-c-captain," the bosun began.

"SMEE!" the captain roared, making the bosun's cheek flush even redder than his bulbous scarlet nose. "How many times am I to tell you that I am never, ever, EVER, to see my own blood?!" As he said this, he rose upwards to his full height, towering above the portly Irishman. Each 'ever' was punctuated by a thunderous step forwards, his boots slamming down on the floorboards. "How many times have I made it explicitly clear that the colour of my blood is the one thing that absolutely, unequivocally, indescribably terrifies me?"

"I-I-I-I-I-I'm s-s-s-s-s-s-sorry, Captain," Smee trembled. "I w-w-w-w-was just about to rem-m-m-m-move it when you woke up."

The captain didn't answer him. Instead, he tore off the bandage, gazing at what lay beneath.

There was a metal casing fixed over the end of his arm. A steel dome, fashioned from a goblet, fastened into the flesh with steel pins. Where the neck of the goblet should have been, a sliver of moonlight curved outwards, a perfect question mark of pointed silver.

"Th-th-th-the doctor fa-fa-fashioned it for you, Captain T—"

"DO NOT CALL ME THAT!" the captain bellowed. He turned, and stalked back to the maps table at the back of his quarters. He stood there for a moment, hunched over the wooden surface, arms supporting him. He dug the point of the hook into the table and pulled, watching the shaving curl upwards as he carved it out. "That is a name that no one knows," he muttered. "That no one fears. I used to be the bosun for the most feared pirate in the world, Smee. The great Edward Thatch. Blackbeard himself! Everybody knows his name! And now, here I am. A captain myself. And nobody knows my name."

"B-b-b-b-but, Captain. If I don't call you that, what do I call you?"

The captain looked at him, fire dancing in his eyes.

"My name shall be one that shall be known by everybody. A name that strikes fear into the heart of all those that hear it. A name, that when that boy—"

“You m-m-m-mean Peter—”

“DO NOT say his name either!” The captain was breathing more and more heavily now. “When that boy, who cheated me, betrayed me, used me, cut off my HAND!” Here, he swiped across the desk with his hook, tearing a thick, ragged line across the surface. "I took him in as a son," he continued, more quietly. "I was the father he never had, I was both mother and father to him. And this is how he repays me? Well, what goes around comes around, Smee. He shall rue the day he met me.”

"A-a-a-and your name, Captain?"

“Yes! When he hears it, he will tremble, as he remembers the day that he first crossed me!”

“And w-w-w-what is this name, C-c-c-captain?”

The captain smiled, tasting the words before he spoke them.

“Why, Smee. What else, but Captain Hook?”

Tick Tock Goes the Croc

What better way to kick off the collection than with an origin story? Tick Tock Goes the Croc (I still think that's one of the best titles I've ever come up with) was a product of another writing competition. This one challenged its participants to retell a well-known fairy tale from the perspective of the antagonist. I decided to turn Peter Pan on its head and make Captain Hook into a sympathetic father figure betrayed by his surrogate son. The rivalry, the animosity, between Pan and Hook is something that is always taken as read; a fact of life. I wanted to explore its origins, see why the two of them are locked in eternal conflict. And then I realised I had a golden opportunity to add backstory to Hook's other antagonist: the crocodile who swallowed his hand. I'll admit, contriving a situation where the crocodile would swallow an alarm clock was somewhat challenging, but I was committed to filling in the backstory, so contrive it I had to. And all in all, this is probably one of my favourite stories in the collection. I've always enjoyed thinking about stories from the perspective of so called 'bad guys', and this story gave me the opportunity to experiment with that idea. After all, good and bad are entirely subjective concepts. That's why I can safely ignore my sister when she says I have bad dress sense.

A Dinner to Die For

The chateau, located just outside the commune of Saussignac in the French Dordogne region, was impressive, imposing and incredible.

The exterior, extending out to his left and right, was more like a palace than a country home, great granite-grey walls, soaring stone spires and sloping slate roofs. Ivy climbed up the wall in a tangled net, nature's last stand against the building that had uprooted it. Craning his neck backwards, Timothy could see three windows rising above each other, each one shuttered and hidden. This may have been only one corner of the castle, but to Timothy, it was like no building he had ever seen before, strikingly set against a background of deep velvet, sprinkled with sequin-like stars. The moon, a ghostly white, full on this New Year's Eve, drifted above him, its pale rays spilling down onto the stone.

"Oi. Move it, Tim, you're blocking us in!" The irritated voice, coming from the open door of the van, was that of his younger sister, Sandra. Timothy hadn't realised that he was still stood in front of the vehicle's sliding door, and that his mother Vanessa, Sandra, Elizabeth, and David were all waiting in the van's cramped rear seating area for him to move so they could disembark. He quickly stepped to one side, hitching his grey rucksack up onto his shoulder. Sandra came out first, glaring at him. Although at fifteen she was two years his junior, Sandra very much liked to believe that she ruled the roost in the family. Next came his mother, wincing slightly as she climbed out and stretched her back. She'd torn a ligament squeezing between two baby car seats when Timothy was still a toddler, and she'd never been able to forget it. Following shortly behind her was young David, aged just fourteen but with the trend and style of a fashionable seventeen-year-old, and his older sister Elizabeth, back from Bristol University to spend New Year with her family.

David and Elizabeth's mother and father, Gregory and Linda Zenopolos, had already climbed out of the front of the minibus and were round the back, fiddling with the rear doors to unload the multitude of suitcases the two families had brought with them.

Timothy heard a door unlocking behind him, and turned to see a rectangle of light opening in the stone wall. A woman stood in the doorway, blonde-haired and slim, a smile set beneath kind eyes. This was Charlotte, the friend who owned the chateau with her husband James. She was wearing a novelty Christmas apron, and Timothy could smell roasting meat drifting through the open door. His mouth watered; he hadn't had much to eat on the plane, and he was very much looking forward to the dinner that was being prepared.

"Greg! Linda! Vanessa!" Charlotte rushed out to greet them. The three adults embraced their hostess, leaving Tim as the only one strong enough to pull the suitcases down from the van.

"Here, Tim, let me help you with that," James said, climbing out of the blue Peugeot that had guided them from the airport. "Ana, go in and make sure nothing's burning while your mother's out here." His daughter, thirteen-year-old Anastasia, slipped past them and through the door, disappearing inside the tower.

"Come right on in out of the cold," Charlotte was saying. "Dinner's not quite ready yet, so why don't you take your things upstairs and freshen up a bit? The kids have a chance to explore the place before the party starts."

"Just watch out for the ghosts," James chuckled, carrying two of the bags over to the door.

"Oh, stop it, James. You'll frighten the little ones," Charlotte replied. Timothy picked up the last two bags and brought them in.

"You're up on the top floor with David," James said, leading Timothy towards the stairs. "I thought you might like to be away from all the girls." Timothy smiled. He and David, despite the three-year age gap between them, and the fact that one lived in England and the other in Cyprus, were the greatest of friends, their bromance legendary throughout the families.

"You lot better take your own cases, 'cause I ain't carrying them all up four flights," Timothy called after the girls, who were already disappearing into the kitchen. Shaking his head, Timothy followed James up the stairs at the back of the living/dining room that they'd come into. The interior, Timothy noted, was just as impressive as the exterior, great stone walls curving upwards, a roaring fire beneath a granite mantlepiece, a long oak table and at least a dozen chairs stretching along the back of the room.

"What's through there?" Timothy asked James, nodding to another passageway leading under the stairs.

"Oh, that. That's the way to the toilet," James replied. "But," he added, a twinkle in his eye, "it used to be the old prison. Used to bring convicts here, leave them to rot. Who knows how many twisted souls perished here." He winked.

The two men made their way up the stairs, passing through an open entrance hall on the first floor, a landing that had been converted into a kind of living room on the second, and into an attic-like space on the third.

"You two'll be staying up here," James said, pointing to a grand room at the end of the passageway. "Where's David?" he asked, turning to look at Timothy.

Timothy shrugged. "Probably checking the place out. Finding the best spot to plug in his PlayStation." He grinned. "That thing's like his life support. It's a miracle he's made it this long without it."

*

As it happened, Timothy was only half right. David was exploring the house, with that natural curiosity that fills all young boys when arriving at a totally new place. However, he was not scouting out either of the first floor living rooms, despite the fact that one had a forty-eight-inch full HD Smart TV. Nor was he stretched out in one of the armchairs on the landing of the second floor, scrolling through his phone, which Timothy might have described as David's defibrillator. He was, in fact, making his way down the passage under the stairs that led to the prison, now the toilet. He'd overheard James mentioning the room's past to Timothy, and his curiosity had been piqued. The passageway was narrow, low, built at a time when nutrition was poor and statures slighter. The toilet was on the left at the end, but David was more interested in the cupboard ahead of him. Although he knew it was impolite, he enjoyed snooping around other people's houses. He had dreams of being a journalist, hopefully in sport, and his natural curiosity was one of his most prominent attributes.

The doors of the cupboard ran from floor to ceiling, dark wood with metal studs. Two ring handles glinted softly in the light from the living/dining room behind him. He took hold of one, twisted the cold metal, and pulled. The door swung open, and he peered inside.

If he was expecting to find anything of interest, he was disappointed. The cupboard was mostly empty, a few rows of shelves with some odds and ends on them. Old glasses and a few rolls of toilet paper, slowly mouldering in the darkness. David turned away.

And then he heard it.

A very faint sound of air whooshing, like someone blowing a dog whistle far away.

David turned, looking back at the cupboard, leaning towards it.

There. He could just feel it. A slight breeze, seemingly emanating from the very wood itself. He put his hand out, and followed the air current, tracing its path back to the cupboard. A knot-hole, almost invisible in the half light, was yawning from the bottom of one of the planks. David's curiosity rose up again. If there was a current, then it wasn't just a stone wall behind this cupboard. He hooked a finger into the hole, and pulled.

The board clicked forward. The cupboard shuddered, and then slid slowly sideways, slightly scraping against the stone floor as it sank into the wall. The passageway continued further on, disappearing into the darkness ahead.

"David? What're you doing?"

It was Anastasia, peering into the passage from the living/dining room. Her slight frame was silhouetted against the light, her small face invisible in the shadow.

"Did you know about this?" David asked, looking back at her. She shook her head.

"I've never seen that before." She hesitated. "Maybe I should get my dad."

"Or maybe we should check it out." He turned back to the circle of blackness, pulling out his phone and turning on the torch app in one practised movement. "Come on." Without waiting for an answer, he turned, and began walking. After a moment's hesitation, Anastasia followed.

The passage ran for only a few metres beyond its original end, but the darkness was so total that David almost didn't realise he had reached the end until he was no more than a foot from it. Sweeping his torch around, he realised that it had branched out into a chamber of some sort, cut into the stone. The room was empty and cold; dead.

The beam picked out a box lying on the floor, thick with dust.

"Ana, come look at this." He beckoned her over as he knelt down beside it. It was wooden, about three feet square, with a hinged lid. David glanced at Anastasia, then flicked the lid up.

Inside, two porcelain-white faces, framed by curling fabric strips, stared up at them. The strips ended in small bells, ones that looked like they hadn't sounded in years. They were lying on a bed of black velvet, the material so dark that they almost seemed to be resting on nothing.

"Masks," David whispered.

Anastasia nodded, feeling fear rising in her stomach. She didn't know why, but something about these masks was making her very, very scared.

"I got an idea," he grinned. "Let's put these on, and jump out and scare the adults at dinner."

"I don't know, David," Anastasia replied, feeling more and more uneasy. "I don't like this. Maybe we should go back."

"Come on, Ana, don't be a baby. It's New Year's Eve. What's that without a little fun and games?" So saying, he reached down, picked up one of the masks, and slipped it over his face.

*

Half an hour later, back in the living/dining room, Charlotte was finishing laying out the New Year's Eve meal. An engorged version of a traditional Christmas dinner to feed ten people, Charlotte had gone above and beyond to feed her guests. Light and dark meat, roasted and creamed potatoes, savoury stuffing and steamed vegetables, all beautifully laid out on the oak surface. A few feet away, by the fireplace, James was telling Timothy about the history of the house.

"And as for the ghosts I mentioned," he smiled over his glass of his glass of red wine, "there was a travelling Italian performance group staying here, sometime in the late eighteenth century. About twenty of them, plus two young children I think. A boy and a girl, if I remember right. They were just passing through, here for just one night before they moved on." He paused, the fire light dancing in his eyes. "But they never left. The whole troupe disappeared, never to be seen again."

"They disappeared?" Timothy asked, a half-smile on his face. He presumed that James was joking.

"Absolutely. They were meant to do two more shows here in France before returning home to Venice, but they never appeared. That's why the locals call this place *'La Château de Disparition'*; the vanishing house."

"Oh James, you love telling that story," Charlotte said, sweeping through with a vase-sized jug of gravy. "Dinner's ready everyone, and we've only got a few minutes left until we ring in the new year, so you better eat fast!"

James went over, picked up a foam-topped beater, and struck the large brass gong that stood in the corner. The sound reverberated around the tower, bouncing off the stone walls all the way to the top floor. The remaining members of the family came scurrying down the stairs, the sound and smell enticing them to leave their armchairs and sofas. Within a minute, there were seven hungry bodies sat around the table, an eighth hurrying out of the kitchen carrying a bottle of wine.

"Where're David and Anastasia?" Gregory asked, glancing around the room.

By way of an answer, Charlotte gave a small shriek, nearly dropping the bottle. The rest followed her gaze, turning towards the passage that led towards the toilet.

Two figures stood at the entrance, hands hanging limply by their sides. They were dressed in the same clothes that David and Anastasia had been wearing, but their faces were different. They were both wearing blank, expressionless masks, pure white, sequinned strips of coloured fabric framing the faces. Timothy recognised the style immediately. They were Venetian; the famous carnival masks that had begun to decline sometime in the eighteenth century.

"There you two are," Charlotte said, trying to recompose herself. "Just in time for dinner. Where on earth did you get those hideous masks from?"

No answer.

The pair just stood there, unmoving, watching the room. The masks were strangely beautiful, the sequins sparkling in the firelight, the faces perfectly smooth and unmarked. And at the same time, Timothy felt a shiver run through him. Something was wrong.

The two children still hadn't moved, and looking closer at them, Timothy felt his heart rate jump up several notches. He'd been peering at the faces, trying to read the expressions of the people wearing them.

But, looking into the small oval holes in the masks, he'd seen no eyes looking back at him.

It wasn't that the eyes were hidden. It wasn't that shadows were obscuring them. The eyes just weren't there.

And now he was looking closer still, he realised that he couldn't see the edges of the masks. There was no lip where the material ended and the skin began. The masks just melted into the flesh. More than that, they were the flesh. There was no distinction.

Timothy felt the icy fingers of fear grip his stomach tight.

The two children stepped forward; arms still limp by their sides. David was moving towards his father, Anastasia towards Charlotte.

"David?" Gregory said, a slight squeak to his voice. His son didn't answer him. Instead, his arm came up, the fist opening slowly. The rest of the table sat in horror, unable to tear their eyes away, as the boy's hand closed around his father's throat.

Outside, the wind howled past the cold stone walls of *la château de disparition*, as, on the stroke of midnight, just as the new year dawned, the vanishing house claimed the first of its newest victims.

A Dinner to Die For

This is one of the few stories I've ever written that was inspired entirely by a place. The setting, a huge old house in the French countryside, was also the writing venue. I was staying with some friends of friends for New Year, and as soon as I saw the building, I knew I had to write something set there. It was just too good a setting to not use. And that being the case, it only seemed fitting to use the family and friends around me as the characters. So, naturally, I decided to write a horror story about my loved ones getting possessed. I've always found Venetian masks to be extremely creepy. My sister had one of them on the wall of her bedroom for a while, and I just could not understand how she could sleep with that thing watching her all night. So I decided to incorporate them into the story, though why there should be two Venetian masks in a French Château is something I still can't really explain.

I think I was originally planning to extend the ending to this one, as I seem to recall having the mental image of one of the characters fleeing up the stairs as the house catches fire, and them being trapped on the top floor as the two possessed children slowly climb up after them. But the inevitable wordcount limit of the competition I was writing for nixed that idea, and I never went back to finish it. And, since I'm committed to these collections capturing the stories as they were written, that ending shall remain consigned to the depths of my mind ... for now.

Blacker Than Black

I got some rules.

Three of 'em, to be exact. Three simple rules for my job, that stop me from screwin' up.

Three simple rules to keep me safe.

Number one: the job comes first. Before family, before friends (not that I got many of either), before anythin'. Don't matter when, don't matter where, don't matter what. I get offered a job, as long as it's legit and doable, I take it. No exceptions.

Number two: the fee. Half up front, half on completion. Non-negotiable. A kinda insurance for each party. Reassures me that the client ain't gonna screw me over and leave me with nothin' but dirt, and reassures the client that I ain't gonna cut and run. Keeps us both invested in the job until it's over. Client don't like my terms, that's their problem. It's my way, or the highway.

And number three: never, ever, look in the box.

These three rules have kept me happy, healthy and wealthy through a long smugglin' career. Well, I say 'long'. Longer than most, anyway. Life expectancy of a professional criminal ain't too long these days. There's clients wantin' to cover their tracks, rival criminals lookin' to cut into whatever I'm carryin', and the Feds, of course. They're all over my ass nowadays. Makes my job a right pain. So inconsiderate.

But, here I am. In the game a solid eight years, and not lookin' to quit any time soon.

Or at least, I wasn't.

But then, I broke my rule.

Now, I'm a dead man walkin'.

In my time, I've smuggled all manner of things, mostly without even knowin' it. Not that I'm duped, God no. But I ain't stupid either. I don't ask about what's in the box, but I do think about where it's comin' from, and where it's goin', and who's likely to be interested. I've run guns from the former Soviet Union to war lords in West Africa. I've flown kilos of cocaine from Columbia and Bolivia right into the US. I've sailed money across the Atlantic from France all the way to Canada.

Those are my guesses. But of course, I wouldn't know anythin' about that. 'Cause I never ask what's in the box. Don't know, don't care. Poachers, drug dealers, thieves. Don't matter who I'm workin' for. They all pay the same. As long as they pay, it don't matter what's in the box.

Or it didn't.

Until this one.

It was a standard job. Nothin' unusual about it. Got the email, encrypted and untraceable. The only stipulations were the words *Handle with care* below the text. Nothin' uncommon about that; clients often want their precious cargo to arrive in one piece. Understandable really. A fairly sizable container, red-painted corrugated metal, the logo *Inductive Logistics* in white on the side. To be picked up at the docks in Jakarta, Indonesia, and sailed over to Darwin in my personal boat, *The Bonny Anne*. Things are often smuggled into Australia via Indonesia these days; makes it easier. A fairly simple journey, a little jaunt around the north-eastern tip of the island of Java, then nothin' but clear skies and plain sailin' south-west across the Indian Ocean into the Timor Sea, before dockin' nice and easy at a private port in Darwin. Only about forty-eight hours. Simple.

Or, it shoulda been.

Until I broke my rule. And I broke it in the worst way.

'Cause I asked what was in the box.

But I didn't ask Them. The "Them", the "They", the client. No, that was what I shoulda done. 'Cause I know exactly what would happen then. Some variation on "What's in the box is none of your concern. You're paid to smuggle, not ask questions." And They would be right. Same thing I been tellin' myself for years and years. Do your job. Don't think about the why, and don't think about the what. Just think about the where, the when, and the how. Just get on with it.

That's what woulda happened if I'd asked Them.

But I didn't ask Them.

I asked myself.

And that was the worst thing I coulda done.

'Cause myself didn't have an answer.

I coulda left it, shoulda left it. Guessed, great. Speculated, sure. Fantasised, fine. Wonder, then deliver and forget it. Drop my load and hit the road, wait for the next job.

But I didn't.

I broke the single most unbreakable rule of smugglin'.

I opened the box.

Some people say that looks can kill. Well, they're damn right. 'Cause this look has killed me.

In my time, I reckon I've smuggled some pretty exotic things. My favourite guesses include diamonds, probably mined by slaves, from Botswana (not much else worth thirty million that can fit in a briefcase), a paintin' stolen from the Louvre (unless whoever stole it decided to keep it locked in their basement right after the story of its theft broke) and, and I'm pretty sure about this one, a live Bengal Tiger from India. That was a fun flight. No matter how loud a turboprop may be, it can't drown out the roars of an airsick big cat. Organs from unwillin' donors, weapons for terrorist groups, even documents for people lookin' for new identities. If it's on the black market, if it's illegal and you can buy it, chances are I've smuggled it.

But there was one thing I never thought I'd smuggle.

And yet, when I opened that door, I found myself lookin' at seven of 'em in the metal container, sat in my boat, in the middle of the Indian Ocean.

I had to let 'em go. I couldn't let 'em finish their journey. Two of 'em didn't look older than eight, and I shudder to think what might have happened to the two women and three girls who were there. Maybe I was wrong. Maybe they were bein' smuggled as refugees, asylum seekers. Maybe they came here voluntarily, lookin' for a better life. Maybe there was someone waitin' to meet 'em at the port, someone who could take 'em somewhere they could make a fresh start, live a good life.

Maybe. But I doubt it.

The inside of the container was filthy. The metal walls were caked in dirt and human waste, the smell hittin' me stronger than any wave had ever done. Even as the boat gently rocked, a small pool of vomit ran down out the open door over my shoes. I didn't care. I barely even noticed. The seven of 'em in there, huddled in the back corner, looked more terrified than anyone I've ever seen. I don't know how long they'd been in there, and I don't know where they came from. Afghanistan or Pakistan, perhaps. They had that kinda look about 'em. They stared at me, and I stared at 'em. There was no sign of any food, any water, or even anywhere for 'em to relieve theirselves. That was how I knew they weren't bein' smuggled in for their own good.

Whoever had put them there, whoever was payin' me to smuggle 'em, they didn't see 'em as people. They were just cargo. Goods. Wares. Property to be bought, smuggled, and sold. Slave labour, prostitution, organ farmin'. Who knows where they coulda ended up.

I ran 'em aground on a beach on East Point, a little peninsula a few miles north of the city of Darwin. I gave 'em all the money I could, then called the police. By the time they turned up, I was long gone. Hopefully they'll treat those people right. Get 'em cleaned up, help 'em find work and shelter. Protect 'em.

So, turns out that years of not carin', of takin' whatever to wherever for whoever, of not thinkin' and just doin', ain't quite enough to destroy a man's conscience. I ain't a good man. I know this. Who knows how many people wouldn't have died or had their lives ruined if I hadn't done my job. But now I seen a different side to the marketplace I been workin' in. Tradin' guns, drugs, artefacts, that's one thing. No different to a regular market. But when you start tradin' in lives, in souls ... that, my friend, is quite another thing. That is where the market becomes blacker than black.

And now, I've traded my own soul. For a look in a box.

They say curiosity killed that cat. Well, draw whiskers on my face and watch me lick my own ass.

I don't even really know who I was workin' for. Could be one of the Mafias, the Triads, the Yakuza, or some other organisation I've never even heard of. Not that it matters. These people. Them. They don't let you go. You can't cross 'em and expect to get away with it. You can't take Their money and then not deliver. Not unless you're either stupid or suicidal.

I never really fancied takin' my own life, and I never considered myself particularly stupid either. Until I opened that damn box, that is. That was stupid. Possibly the most stupid thing I've done in my life.

I knew I had to get gone after I saw the same guy walk past my house in Austin three times in one afternoon. I'll give the dude credit; he was very sneaky about it. He was draggin' a wheeled bag behind him, wearin' a baseball cap and shades. The bag was full of magazines, and he stopped at each door to slip one of the glossy bundles of lies and rumours through each person's mail slot. The white wires of his headphones twisted down to his pocket, and I could see his head noddin' slightly to the beat as I watched him through the window, makin' his way first down my side of the street, then back up the other side.

His mistakes? There were three. First, he was too old to be doin' that job. That's a job for a kid lookin' to earn a few bucks, not a full-grown adult. Second, he walked past my window one too many times. He'd done both sides of the street. He hadn't needed to come back. But he had. And that was set my suspicions goin'.

His third was the one that really told me to get the hell outta there as fast as I could. He'd stopped outside my house on his third trip past, next to where my pickup was parked in the driveway. He was crouched down behind the car, fiddlin' with somethin' close to the ground, maybe tyin' his shoelaces or somethin'. But he didn't know I could see his reflection in the mirror over the truck's dashboard. It weren't his laces he was messin' with. It was somethin' with wires and tape and a small package. It weren't hard to work out what he was doin'.

And so I got the F out of T faster than a Frenchman after hearin' a gunshot. That's why I'm currently hidin' in the bushes next to an airfield in Virginia, with a pistol in my back pocket and a backpack stuffed with dollars over my shoulder. I can see my plane sittin' in the garage. She's an old turboprop, my *Mary Read*, but she's taken me all over the world, and she's never let me down yet. It's risky to take her; if They knew where I lived, They probably know about my plane too. Coulda left anythin' that could kill me. But let's be real, I was dead from the moment I decided to break my rule.

I've smuggled so many things from so many places for so many people. I've lied, bribed, threatened and coerced my way across more borders than I could count. I've slipped through so many loopholes I shoulda started a side business as a lawyer. I must have smuggled just about everythin' that anyone could ever want or need.

But I never thought I'd have to smuggle myself.

Blacker Than Black

This story is one that's had a couple of different versions over the years. It was originally written to explore the theme of "Markets" for the Olga Sinclair Short Story Competition (although sadly it was not as successful as Strangers on a Train). I wanted to try and look at a different kind of market to the traditional kind that Norwich is famous for. The black market, then, seemed like a logical fit. Credit where credit is due, part of the inspiration for this story comes from the Alex Rider book Snakehead, where Alex has to be smuggled out of Indonesia and into Australia.

From the original competition draft, I extended and adapted the story for one of my university pieces, and then I redrafted it one last time because I liked it. It was a fun challenge to think of all the different things someone might need smuggled from place to place. But then I landed on people, and I knew I had to make that the focus of my story. People smuggling, as far as I can see, is one of the most morally questionable things someone can do, particularly if there's a chance they're being smuggled for something unpleasant. This led to the idea of the regretful smuggler who tries to detach himself from his work, but just can't escape from his feelings about this particular cargo.

Our nameless narrator quickly became one of my more interesting characters, at least in my mind. He has rules to keep himself safe, then he breaks his own rules and has to face the consequences. But were the rules there to protect his physical safety, or his moral integrity?

Island Retreat

We didn't mean to come to the island.

It was an accident, a mistake, a misunderstanding; a series of unfortunate events, one might say. Yet here we are.

At least our holiday started well.

Two guys, three girls. A week's cruise around the Caribbean. Sun, sea, swimming, sipping, secrets and seductions. What could go wrong?

As it turns out, a lot.

I'm still not sure what he's done to us is legal. I could be wrong, but I'm fairly certain maritime laws from the early eighteenth century don't still apply. Not that that would have stopped Captain Teach anyway. He was so mad you could have cooked a seagull on his face. As long as you didn't mind a few eyebrow or moustache hairs on it.

Captain Ulysses Nelson Teach had very proudly told us when we stepped onto his ship that his very first breath had been the salty tang of sea air, and so had every breath since. A born sailor, from a family of sailors, from a village that had made its living on sailing and fishing. However, he was the only one to have crossed the Atlantic to America before dropping anchor and settling down. Now, he took folks like us around the islands on pleasure cruises, still enjoying the wind in his hair and the spray on his lips. He'd assured us that he had been born at, lived at and would die at sea.

Well, it looks like we may have a similar fate.

It really was an accident, although, admittedly, Oliver really should have been more careful. But sometimes, things just happen. A friendly conversation on the ship's foredeck with the Captain's wife Aurora, and one choppy wave later, what was in fact the noble act of trying to catch her, ends with the Captain seeing Oliver holding his wife, his right hand against her breast. He didn't mean for it to be there; it was just an accident. Yet an hour later, we're sat on a beach on our own, watching *Le Transfuge* sail away into the sunset. At least they let us get our bags from the cabins.

We've been here two days now, long enough for us to scout out the island so we can see exactly what kind of place we've been marooned on. To put it bluntly, we're screwed. There's a small pool of fresh water in the middle of the island, but there's no telling what kind of parasites and diseases are floating around in there, and we've got no way of boiling it. I mean, we were expecting a relaxing Caribbean cruise, not an improvised island retreat. There's maybe enough sun cream to last the five of us about a month (we all stocked up just before we left, thankfully), but no more. None of us have got more than a couple of snacks in our suitcases, and just a few small bottles of water. And a bottle of whisky that I was saving for a special occasion.

I look back towards the makeshift bundle of loose branches and trees we've been using as shelter, shaking my head wearily. The thing is about one strong fart away from being reduced to matchsticks. None of us have any clue about how to survive on an island like this. Sure, we watched *Castaway*. We saw Tom Hanks find a way to beat the odds and stay alive on an island very much like this one. I think Ed might even have read *Robinson Crusoe* at school, and I was a Boy Scout when I was a kid. But really, we've got no idea. The shelter was a product of guesswork and half remembered childhood memories of building forts in the nearby forests, and I've seen Jenga towers that look more stable.

We've thought about ways of calling for help, sure. But there's not much to be done. We've all got phones, but they're at the mercy of a dwindling power supply and only a splash away from being useless. Well, being completely useless. No signal out here anyway. I think Tania might have a portable charger, but there's really no point, and we all know it. We considered trying to make some sort of burning SOS on the beach for any planes flying overhead to see, but we don't have any way to light it. Besides, the beach is so small the letters wouldn't be big enough to read from the top of a palm tree, let alone from thirty-three thousand feet. Sally has a hand mirror in her bag that we could use to signal a passing ship, but that relies on there being a passing ship to signal.

So, at the risk of sounding like a broken record: we're screwed.

"Hey! Charlie! You're gonna want to see this!" It's Lucy, calling me from down the beach, breaking my train of thought. I stand up, brushing sand off my shorts, and head along the water's edge, feeling the saltwater wash over my feet. At least he dropped us somewhere that, in other circumstances, could be the definition of a tropical paradise. Pure white beaches, a beautifully clear turquoise ocean, palm trees lining the beach. All you need are some sun loungers and a Pina Colada and you've got an ideal holiday destination.

Too bad it'll end up being our graveyard.

I find Lucy and the other two girls standing at the edge of the thick foliage that dominates the centre of the island, staring down at the ground. I'm about to ask where Ollie got to, when suddenly he appears from among the trees, arms full of hairy brown balls. He staggers over to where we're standing, and unceremoniously dumps his cargo on the sand.

"Coconuts!" he announces, very pleased with himself.

I shake my head. "Great," I say. "So now we can go full Tom Hanks and make ourselves imaginary friends."

"They're good for drinking, smart ass," Ollie replies. "And I think I read somewhere that you can eat the flesh inside if you can get it out."

"So ... How do we do that?" I ask. "Sit here and play a game of 'Coconut, Coconut, Coconut, Crack!'?"

Lucy shakes her head. "Charlie, with a head as thick as yours, we can just crack them on your forehead."

I give her a playful punch on the arm. Lucy, Oliver, Sally, and Tania. I wonder if anyone will ever work out where we five have gone, what happened to us. I somewhat doubt it. This island is small enough for you to walk around in an hour, probably no more than two kilometres from one side to the other. Too small to appear on any maps, too small for anyone to notice.

"What was it you said I had to see?" I ask, wrinkling my nose slightly.

"Look," Ollie gestures to the ground. A small mound of brown, rounded pellets lies just outside the treeline, its pungent odour reaching my nostrils.

"You brought me over here to show me where we're starting a toilet?" I ask, incredulous. "Do I even wanna ask whose it is?"

"No, you moron!" Tania shakes her head. "It's not one of ours."

"So?" I ask. "You dragged me down here for a literal shitshow?"

"Think about it," Tania responds. "It's not one of ours, so something else did it. It's still fresh. So ..."

I finally make the connection.

"There're other animals here." My stomach adequately demonstrates the result of the next thought, and we all laugh.

"Maybe there's hope after all," I say.

"Provided Ogling Ollie can keep his hands off them," Sally teases, digging him in the ribs. Ollie blushes a deep scarlet, keeping his eyes fixed on the ground.

"I told you, it was an accident," he mumbles.

"Honestly Ollie, if you were that desperate to cop a feel you could have just asked!" Sally continues, laughing along with the rest of us. Ollie maintains an embarrassed silence, suddenly fascinated by the droppings they discovered. His ears have gone as red as his face, which would put most prime tomatoes to shame.

Maybe this won't be so bad, after all. I mean, the situation's not great. That's a given. But now there's hope. We've got something to drink, potential food, and surely someone will start asking questions when we don't come back with Captain Crunch. And even if worst comes to worst, at least I'm here with these guys. Strong, silent Ollie; smart, stable Tania; Lucy, warm and wacky; and flirty Sally, cheeky and comedic. We've known each other for years. We've laughed together, drunk together, cried together, worked together, fought together, even slept together. Now it seems we might even die together.

And I can't think of anyone with whom I'd rather spend my final days.

Well, that was an odd mix of humour and bleakness wasn't it? In truth, I have no idea where this story came from. This was the product of one of my many sleepless nights during my first year at university, so the original inspiration has been lost in the blur that those days have merged into in my mind. So I guess it's time to analyse my own writing like the self-obsessed pretentious writer that I'm supposed to be. I think I was trying to illustrate the idea that human beings try to stay optimistic even in moments of hopelessness. By juxtaposing impending death with a sarcastic, somewhat humorous tone, the reader really gets a sense of ... Yeah, I'm gonna level with you, I really don't know what my goal was here. I can see what I did and what effect it creates, but I can't remember why I did it. It's a very weird feeling, but I still kinda like this story. I did enjoy the fact that the initials of the friends spell out "LOST". And that Captain Teach's unusually long name spells out... well, I'll let you check that one. Nice touch, past me.

Oh God, I really am that kind of self-congratulatory writer.

A Blend of Snow and Blood

The tree was the only thing that broke the otherwise flat landscape. It stood alone, leafless and naked, its branches twisted and bare. The snow lay unbroken on the ground and swirled thickly through the air, any distinction between the two impossible in the maelstrom of white. The tree, its wood black and knotted, almost appeared to be floating in a sea of white, as if the storm had pulled it from the ground and tossed it skyward to float eternally among the clouds.

The paw that crunched into the snow was wide and flat, the fur covering it a deep brown. Flakes had settled among the dark hairs and frozen them together, creating rigid clumps that stuck out like spines. As the bear took another step onward, it left behind a frying pan sized indentation in the snow, the latest of many that stretched back through the whiteness. The creature was huge, more than six feet high at the shoulder and stretching almost eleven feet from snout to stubby tail. Stood on its hind legs, it would have towered above even the tallest man. Its size was exacerbated still further by the dwarf riding on its back.

Törven Dobrac peered through the white curtain that hung and danced before him, obscuring everything. His cheeks and nose had long since passed into unfeelingness, his fingers only spared by the thick leather gloves that gripped the deep fur at the bear's neck. Ice had stiffened his red beard, a frozen inverted flame that swung from his chin like a bell. A hood, lined with wool and several inches thick, covered the top of his head, the cowl hanging down over his forehead. He knew he had to be going the right way. Snowstorms made navigating by map impossible, and even the sailor's method of using the stars was out of the question. But it held no power over the compass that was affixed to the saddle he was perched upon, the bright red needle vibrant in the blinding white. As long as he kept heading north, he wouldn't stray far.

He reached down and checked the straps that ran down Noha's sides, coming together under her warm belly. They were still secure, the leather frozen stiff but holding firm. He relaxed a fraction. There was still time. The package was secure, and the storm appeared to be easing off the tiniest bit.

And then he heard the howls.

Just one at first. Then another. Within five seconds, there were six distinct voices calling through the white air, the sound piercing and chilling. Törven's heart began to thump in his ears. Beneath him, Noha tensed, sensing the danger. She hardly needed the encouragement of Törven yelling, "Go!" before she was off, battling through the driving snow, wind tearing at her eyes and racing through her fur.

Törven gripped the bear's fur tighter as she lumbered along, past the tree that stood like an empty gallows, its boughs dead and gnarled. He could hear the howls still sounding behind them, a call and response conversation that steadily grew louder. He knew that Noha, try as she might, could not outrun them, not with him on her back.

He made a quick decision, then pulled on the fur and brought her to a confused stop. Grabbing his bag from its place on the saddle, he hooked one foot into the ladder that hung down the bear's side, descending rapidly until his boots crunched into the snow. Stood at ground level, the top of his head barely reached her knee. Noha looked round at him, concern in her eyes. Törven walked forward, and gently stroked her snout, looking into the beautiful hazel eyes behind it.

"I need you to go on ahead, Noha," he said softly. Despite the shrieking wind, his voice was low and gentle. "I'll stay here and hold him off. That should give you enough time to make it out of this storm and back to the castle."

Noha moaned, a deep and awful sound full of sorrow. She'd understood every word, but didn't want to listen to it.

"It's the only way. You know that. If he gets his hands on her, who knows what he'll unleash. You have to go now, girl." He smiled; a sad smile, a knowing smile. "I'll miss you, Noha. But it has to be done." He leaned forward, and gently kissed the bear's cheek, burying his face in her thick fur. Noha groaned one last time, nuzzling up to Törven.

"Go on, girl. Get her home safe."

Noha gave him a final look, then threw back her head and roared. A long, loud, heartrending roar. The sound of an animal in pain. And then, she was off, thundering through the snow and disappearing as if a curtain had been drawn.

Törven turned and began to make his way back in the direction they'd come, following the prints left by Noha's huge paws. With his right hand, he reached under his thick leather jacket and drew out a dagger. The weapon was elegantly simple, a silver blade and a fabric-wrapped handle, devoid of any fancy ornamentation. As he gripped it in his gloved hand, he muttered a few words in a language long ago lost to obscurity. The silver crosspiece of the dagger began to glow faintly, the light wrapping itself around Törven's hand. When the glow faded, a sphere of metal remained, joined to a steel band encircling the dwarf's wrist. Even with numbing fingers and thick gloves hindering his dexterity, it was now impossible for Törven to drop the dagger.

He saw a dark shape stalking towards him from out of the white haze. It moved slowly, confidently, with the air of a hunter closing in on its prey. A second later, two more appeared. Then another two. They were all grey, their coats thick and matted from the wind. Their eyes were yellow or ice-blue, full of cold pleasure. One drew back its lips into a snarl, exposing the curving teeth, more yellow than white, set in gums of the palest pink.

A laugh drifted by on the breeze, dancing among the snowflakes and circling around Törven's head. It was a terrible, hollow laugh, empty of any humour or warmth.

"I know you're here, Kaldion!" Törven called out to the emptiness. "Show yourself."

"As you wish." The words, spoken from nowhere, sent a shiver racing down the dwarf's spine.

A figure stepped out of nothing, the white simply forming into a hooded man. The man was clad in robes that were every bit as colourless as the landscape around him. Little of his face could be seen behind the long cowl, pointed like an eagle's beak, but the lips were pale and bloodless, the skin around them like that of a corpse. The figure floated a foot above the ground, his feet touching nothing but the snowflakes that darted around them. He raised a skeletal hand, a single bony finger pointed towards Törven.

"You have something of mine, dwarf." His words were somehow colder than the frozen air around them, each word sending goosepimples racing over Törven's skin. "Return it to me."

"She is not yours," Törven shot back defiantly. "You cannot have her."

"Do not stand in my way," the necromancer warned. "I will have that girl."

"Then go. Take her." Törven spread his arms wide. "But I will give every last drop of blood in my veins, every breath of air in my lungs, every beat of my heart, to ensure that you will never lay a finger on her."

Kaldion smiled a chilling, terrifying smile.

"I believe you."

The sixth wolf, larger than all the others, flew over the wizard's head, a black shape with red eyes that seemed to suck all light into its colourless fur. Its jaws opened in a terrible snarl as its fangs reached for the dwarf's head, ready to tear flesh from bone.

They found only empty air.

Törven had reacted with incredible speed, rolling forwards underneath the leaping creature. As he came out of the roll, he reached upward with the dagger, feeling a surge of satisfaction as the tip cut into the underbelly of the wolf. Blood pattered down into the snow, the only spots of colour in an otherwise empty landscape.

Törven turned to face the other five who were closing in on him, angered by the injury to their alpha. Another one charged him, snapping at his legs. Törven landed a square kick to its muzzle, knocking it aside as he brought the blade down. The silver flashed through the grey fur, splitting the skin beneath it and sending a gushing geyser of red bursting forth from a severed artery. The wolf howled, staggering around in the snow before collapsing onto its side.

The dwarf, deceptively agile even in the thick snow, danced around another two who tried to come at him from different sides, spinning left around them with elegant ease. Before the closest one could stop him, he'd leapt up onto its back, grabbing hold of the scruff of its neck. The creature's legs couldn't support the added weight of Törven's stocky frame, and gave out, sending the two crashing into the snow. Törven grabbed the wolf's muzzle with his left hand, clamping its jaws shut. He snaked his other arm around the animal's neck, and wrenched the two limbs in opposite directions. There was a stomach-churning crunch as its neck broke, and it stopped struggling.

Törven stumbled back to his feet, only to be knocked flat on his back by the alpha. Its paws landed square on his shoulders, pinning his arms to the ground. Its huge weight bore down upon him, pressing him into the snow. He struggled desperately, trying to free his arms, but it was no use. The wolf leaned down towards him, its clouding breath blowing into his face. It carried the smell of death itself. Törven could see the cruelty in the creature's eyes, the satisfaction of the kill.

One second later, and that look was gone.

Törven brought his boot back down, the three-inch blade protruding from the toe now slick with lupine blood. Activated by curling his toes in the right way, the hidden weapon had saved his life more times than he could count. The black wolf let out a howl of anguish, staggering sideways. With his arms freed, Törven lunged upwards with his dagger. The blade plunged into the soft flesh underneath the wolf's chin, and carried on up, finally lodging itself in the base of the brain. The alpha gave a dreadful cry, and collapsed. Törven did the opposite, forcing himself back to his feet as the other three wolves stalked towards him together.

He was trapped.

He couldn't focus on any one of them without the others coming at him. He couldn't run, or they would all get him.

So he chose the third option.

In a single fluid movement, his left arm reached over his shoulder, grasping the wooden stock that protruded from behind his head, his gloved finger sliding through the metal ring. Before the wolves could move, he'd pulled the weapon free, brought it round and, resting it on his right forearm, fired.

The blunderbuss roared impossibly loudly, drowning out the moaning wind for a split second. The metal balls tore through the three wolves, ripping through their hide and sending them tumbling over themselves before coming to rest in the snow, red slowly spreading around the corpses.

Törven allowed himself a brief feeling of pleasure, but froze when he heard a soft roaring from behind him. He tried to turn and dodge but he was much too late.

The ball of black fire caught him square in the back, sending him cartwheeling forward to faceplant in the snow. He couldn't move. His world was spinning, his body screaming from every nerve.

"An impressive performance, Törven." The voice of Kaldion, soft, mocking, coming from a mile away. "But all in vain. I'll have that girl, and my revenge. And you? Nothing, but an icy grave." The necromancer gave another terrible laugh that faded away into the wind as he turned and stepped into nothingness.

Törven tried to get up, but the effort was too much. Around him, white darkened, passing from grey to charcoal and finally, peacefully, into black.

*

Warmth.

That was the first thing Törven became aware of as his mind slowly thawed out of the frost of unconsciousness. Not a faint, indistinct feeling, but an enveloping, loving heat, like a mother's arms wrapped around him. Slowly, he cracked his eyes open, fully expecting snowflakes to sting his eyeballs. But none came. Light, soft and mellow rather than harsh and white, filled his vision, soothing away the darkness that clouded his mind. As strength returned to his muscles, he gently propped himself up, and looked around him.

He was lying on a bed in a small, comfortable room, the walls bare brown rock. There was a chair set in the corner, on which his leather coat and breeches were laid. His thick boots sat neatly beneath the seat. His dagger, blunderbuss and bag sat patiently on a table beside the chair. There were no windows and no obvious source of heat or light. Rather, the air itself seemed to radiate energy, as if it were alive with microscopic flames.

Törven slipped out of bed, his thick woollen socks hitting a stone floor that should have been cold, but instead was pleasantly warm. He could hear no sounds from outside the wooden door before him, so quickly dressed again, sliding his equipment back into its holsters. As he turned to leave, the door suddenly opened, seemingly of its own accord.

"Wait, Carrier." The gentle words came from nowhere, the very air itself seeming to speak.

"Who are you?" Törven called out, more than a little unnerved. "Where am I?"

"We are the Zimnae," came the response.

"The Zimnae? The snow spirits?" Törven shook his head. "I thought you were just a myth."

"We have allowed ourselves to fall out of memory, so that we may go unnoticed."

The words filled the air around him, coming from everywhere and nowhere.

"You saved me. Why?"

"Kaldion must not be allowed to claim the Culzo. If he does, he will raise an army of the dead, and lay waste to the land. You and your beast must reach the castle safely with the Culzo. If not, nothing, living or dead, will be safe."

"How can I defeat him? He's an undead sorcerer of immense power. I'm nothing more than a messenger."

"You must look to your heart, Carrier. There will you find the power you seek."

"That doesn't make any sense! What do you mean?" But the spirits provided no answers.

"You must go now, Carrier. Your beast struggles onwards, but Kaldion grows ever closer. We can help to hold back the storm from your path, but the necromancer's magic is strong. You must hurry. Farewell, noble Törven. May the winds carry you ever onwards."

The words died away, and the air seemed to vibrate, the energy pulsing through it growing stronger and more intense until it had built to a light that was all consuming. Then, suddenly, it was gone, replaced by the harsh whiteness of the blizzard. The snow lashed down at him, stinging his cheeks once more.

The dwarf turned, and saw a sight that made his heart leap. A large, dark shape was lumbering through the white towards him, fighting through the driving wind. A familiar roar rumbled through the gale to reach his ears as Noha barrelled towards him, the joy visible in her eyes as she reached him, nearly knocking him over as she nuzzled her head into him, moaning happily.

"Hello, girl," Törven grinned, rubbing her behind the ears. "I never thought I'd see you again." Noha looked down at him, her eyes saying that she had thought the same. She opened her impossibly large jaws, and gently licked his face, leaving him wiping spittle from his bulbous nose.

"I missed you too, Noha," he smiled. "But we have to move on. Kaldion is coming, and we have to get her back to the castle." Törven swung his foot into the ladder, scrambled onto Noha's broad back, and patted her thick neck. The bear roared, and thundered off through the snowstorm. As they went, Törven noticed that there almost seemed to be a corridor opening up before them, the swirling flakes darting out of their way, and he remembered the words of the Zimnae. He smiled, held tightly onto Noha's fur, and urged her onward, through the white, and toward civilisation.

They almost made it.

It didn't seem fair to Törven. He could see where the snow and the storm ended, where rocks and grass poked through the thinning carpet. He could feel a warmer breeze, see the sun peaking from behind clouds. Squinting into the distance, he could just make out the spires of the castle, see the banner flying from the tower.

And yet, floating before them, unfurling himself from the last of the whiteness, was Kaldion.

"You!" the necromancer spat at Törven, a voice poisoned with hatred. "How are you alive?"

"I had some help from some new friends." Törven was already unsheathing his dagger and muttering the incantation, feeling the metal wrap itself around his wrist.

"The Zimnae." Kaldion's eyes narrowed with loathing. "My master told me he'd destroyed them all years ago. But I always wondered if any managed to survive. No matter. They cannot save you now."

As he spoke, he raised his hands to the sky, bony fingers splayed. The snow swirled around him, the flakes darting about his arms. Then, suddenly, he shouted to the sky, his voice cutting through the shrieking of the storm. The words were alien, incomprehensible, and yet filled with an unmistakable evil. As he did so, he flung his arms out, palms flat, pointing in opposite directions.

Törven felt the blast wash over him, felt it tug at his beard and at Noha's fur. The force of the spell, quite literally, blew the storm away. In an instant the air was cleared, the snowflakes that had choked it suddenly banished. The clouds that obscured the sun fled, letting light pour down onto the figures who faced each other. Snow still clung to the ground in a deep carpet, but otherwise it could have been a bright midsummer's day.

"Your spirit friends will help you no more, dwarf," the wizard chuckled. "Now, you die."

Törven unzipped his jacket with his free hand, knowing he would soon overheat in the thick garment. He slung it across the saddle, peeled off his left glove, restrapped his blunderbuss to his back, and dismounted from the bear.

"Stand aside, Kaldion," he ordered, doing his best to keep the fear out of his voice. "The child will never be yours."

"That, my vertically challenged friend, is where you are wrong." Kaldion's face cracked into a ghastly grimace of a smile. "The girl, and this land, will kneel before me. The one true lord of both the living and the dead. You will not stand in my way ... But," he continued, with a hint of warmth creeping into his voice, "if you turn her over to me now, I will allow you and your ..." he glanced distastefully at Noha, who was growling softly, hackles raised, eyes narrowed, "pet," he concluded, "to live."

"Is there anyone who trusts the word of a corpse?" Törven shook his head.

"But Törven, is it not said that dead men tell no lies?"

"You may be dead, Kaldion. But you're no man. Not anymore." Törven raised his dagger. "I will never give you that child."

"Then I will take her from your bear's moaning corpse!"

Törven hadn't even seen Kaldion form the flames in his hand, but the black ball was speeding through the air towards him before he knew what was happening. He had no time to react, no time to get out of the way.

But the ball never reached him.

Half a foot from his chest, the dark flames burst apart, dissipating harmlessly into the air.

For a moment, nobody moved. Both men were too stunned to react, unable to understand what had happened.

It was like a snowball being thrown against a stone wall. One second the sphere of death had been hurtling through the air. The next, it simply exploded, the last flickering flames twisting and disappearing in the blink of an eye.

"Impossible," Kaldion whispered. "How? HOW?" he howled at the sky.

Törven, for his part, didn't have an answer. He was completely shocked, unable to comprehend how he had just avoided death.

That was when he felt something cool pressing against his chest, just to the left of his sternum. He fumbled for the inside pocket of his tunic, and felt something had been slipped inside, something he hadn't noticed until now.

It was a snowflake.

A single, frozen snowflake, paper thin but the size of his palm. He could feel the coolness of the ice beneath his fingers. Despite its apparent fragility, the ice felt as hard and solid as steel; firm and ungiving.

"Look to your heart," he muttered, understanding now what the Zimnae had meant by their words. They had given him a tool, a charm, to protect him from Kaldion's magic.

Kaldion roared in anger, a furious wind rushing around him. As Törven watched, the white robed figure grew in size, spine stretching, arms and legs lengthening, until he stood at least eight feet tall and three feet white, a giant of a man before the dwarf.

"Damn you and your damn fairies!" he screamed. "I will have that child!" The wizard raised his arms, palms upwards, and thundered out another spell, this one long and more terrifying than the last. The ground around Törven's feet began to rumble and shake, the vibrations travelling up his legs. Beside him, Noha whimpered, sensing the dangerous unnaturalness that was to come.

A skeletal hand burst through the ground, fingers that were more grey than white reaching for the sky. It was rapidly followed by another, and then three more. Within ten seconds, there were five reanimated corpses, each in various states of decay, standing around Törven and Noha. Their eyes (in those that still had them) were empty, staring, no emotion or feeling behind them. They had been resurrected as nothing more than puppets, mindless drones with only one task: kill.

Kaldion flicked his wrists out, spitting out one final incantation. The air before his hands instantly froze, forming a long, icicle-like sword in his left hand, a shield of solid ice on his right wrist. The ice was a terrible, empty blue, the colour of death.

"Go! Bring me the child!" Kaldion commanded, pointing towards Noha with his sword. As one, the undead servants lumbered towards the bear. They made no sound, nor showed any emotion.

Törven readied his dagger, but before he could attack the first of the shambling minions, the giant Necromancer came at him, swinging his icy blade in great scything arcs. Törven dodged and rolled away, narrowly avoiding a strike that would, had it connected, have split his torso open lengthways. He came out of the roll and back onto his feet, already shifting his weight to lunge forward with the dagger. The dwarf's nimbleness and agility caught the necromancer by surprise. In his larger form the wizard was much slower, and was unable to bring his shield down in time to prevent Törven's blade sliding between his ribs.

Blood, black rather than red, bubbled from the wound and dropped to the snow. But Kaldion barely seemed fazed.

"How can you kill a dead man, dwarf?" He grinned, slamming the shield forward into Törven's face. The hard, flat ice impacted with incredible force, knocking Törven back. He stumbled, his nose flattened, blood of his own streaming over his face and into his beard. He blinked back tears, knowing with a sick certainty that, while he had landed what should have been a fatal blow, it had done nothing to his opponent.

Meanwhile, Noha was taking on the five skeletal warriors. Had they been capable of feeling anything, they might have been utterly terrified at the roar that she let out, the sound tearing across the landscape through the now clear air, bouncing off hillsides and echoing through distant caves. She brought up one giant paw, claws like sickles protruding from between the toes, and swiped at the nearest of the shuffling creatures. The corpse was knocked aside like a ragdoll, deep gashes torn across its face and neck. Any man would have been killed by such a blow. Indeed, the force was strong enough to partially detach the thing's head from its neck, leaving a great rip in the flesh. But the unwilling servant simply picked itself back up and came at her again.

Noha roared in disbelief, then launched herself at another two who were marching side by side. One massive forepaw pinned each of them to the ground, ribs cracking under the immense weight. But again, the two figures seemed unperturbed. One reached up and slashed at Noha's chest with fingers that had lost all their flesh. The bone scratched the flesh beneath the thick fur, sending a few droplets of blood pattering to the snow. Noha roared, then sprang forward, jaws yawning open to then close around the torso of another possessed body. Her teeth, each one as long and sharp as a dagger, sliced easily through the decaying flesh and closed around the spine. Holding the body against the floor with her paws, she pulled upward, ripping a section of the bony column out with a hideous tearing sound. Now, only a thin band of flesh connected the upper and lower parts of the thing's body. It tried to stand, but its top half flopped sideways, pulling its legs back to the floor.

Törven saw none of this, as he frantically tried to avoid Kaldion's onslaught of stabs and slashes. The huge figure was relentless, attacking from every angle, using the shield to try and cut off the dwarf's evasive manoeuvres, forcing him to back away through the snow. He was tiring, and the magician knew it. The snow impeded his movements, his nose was still streaming blood, and the dagger was feeling heavier and heavier in his hand.

He tried to switch it up and go on the offensive, but it was hopeless. Kaldion easily turned the blade aside with his shield, the razor-sharp tip not even scratching the ice. The necromancer followed it up with a strike from his sword hand, the hilt of the weapon slamming into Törven's head. The dwarf was knocked onto his back, crying out. Before he could recover, Kaldion darted forward, raised his blade, and brought it down.

The ice passed cleanly through Törven's forearm, just below the elbow. The dagger, still wrapped around the wrist, fell into the snow. Törven screamed, a terrible, horrible scream. Blood gushed from the severed limb, steaming as it hit the snow, staining it a deep crimson. Above him, Kaldion laughed.

"I appear to have 'disarmed' you," he gloated. "Next it will be your bear. And then, the kingdom." He raised his icicle blade above his head, the blue shining terribly in the sunlight. "Goodbye, Törven."

The blade began to plunge down.

Then, suddenly, Noha barrelled into Kaldion out of nowhere. The wizard was caught completely by surprise. The bear's full bulk powered into him, knocking him to the ground. The sword was sent flying, spinning away into the snow. Kaldion hit the ground beside Törven, struggling as Noha tore at his face with her teeth and carved chunks from his chest with her claws. But even this could not hurt him mortally. He was, after all, past mortality. With a snarl, he pushed the bear off him, sending the mighty beast rolling over the ground. He pulled himself to his feet, and stalked over to her as she lay on her side. He could see wounds across her chest and sides where his minions had attacked her. A shame they had been unable to retrieve the bundle that he could see strapped to her belly.

"And now, you are mine," he whispered to the bundle.

"No she's not."

Even as Kaldion spun round, Törven thrust forward with his remaining left hand. In it was clutched the enchanted snowflake the Zimnae had given him. It was much too late for Kaldion to react. The snowflake connected with his forehead, and burned there.

The necromancer screamed, a terrible, howling, wailing scream of pure anguish. He thrashed around, hands tearing at his brow. Something terrible was happening to his body. The flesh was rotting and falling off before Törven's eyes, as if some terrible disease were eating away at it. His robes now hung off bones, his eyes staring out of skull.

The skeleton opened its mouth as if to utter one last spell.

And then it collapsed into the snow.

Törven collapsed beside him. Blood still pumped from his recent amputation, but he no longer felt anything. No pain, no suffering, no anger. Instead, he just felt tired.

So very, very tired.

Noha came over to him, nuzzling gently at him.

"Thank you, girl," he whispered. "Thank you."

Noha moaned, her eyes filled with sadness.

"Go on. Get to the castle. Get her home."

Noha howled, a pain-filled howl that seemed to split the very air.

"Leave me. Take her home. Take her ..."

Törven's eyes closed.

He never felt the jaws that closed gently around his midriff. Nor did he feel the jolts and judders of the beast that carried him; charging across the countryside, looking for someone to help save a life.

A Blend of Snow and Blood

Yeah, the title might be a little Game of Thronesy *(if that's a thing), but let's be real, all fantasy writing sprawls over itself a little bit. Let's not even begin to get into how much George R.R. Martin might have cribbed from J.R.R. Tolkein (though those middle initials might be a good start). Besides, the main influence for this story isn't actually a book, or a TV show for that matter. It was, of course, a video game.* World of Warcraft, *to be specific.*

I never got properly into WoW *in the way some people did, the way which earned it its reputation of a second job where you have to pay to go to work; but I did play it a bit, especially when I was younger. One of the original cinematics for the game showed a red-bearded dwarven hunter with a blunderbuss stood beside a huge bear in the middle of a blizzard. For some reason, that image stuck with me. And when the time came to write a fantasy story, that was what I started with. I wanted to try and hold onto the sense of mystery that fantasy inherently creates. That's why I never explain who the child strapped to Noha's stomach is, what she can do, or why Torven was tasked with escorting her. I wanted the reader to be engaged almost entirely with what was happening in the story, without needing to stop and question the context. Fantasy, after all, is supposed to be about letting go of reason and rationality, and simply enjoying a world beyond our own.*

Shadows in the Moonlight

A flicker in the night.

A dark shadow, barely noticeable, dancing at the corner of your vision.

There's nothing there.

Of course there's nothing there. You're alone, on the street at night, on the way home.

But there's nothing worse than being alone, and feeling like you're not alone.

You turn, hurry along onwards. The house is just around the corner, you can almost see it.

A rustle in the bushes. You stop dead.

A black cat darts out of the shrubbery and across the road.

You shake your head, looking back up at the road.

Then, all is black.

Shadows in the Moonlight

Another foray of mine into the world of micro-fiction, Shadows in the Moonlight *is a subtle return of our good friend,* The Man Who Isn't There. *Micro-fiction is a real challenge for me as someone who tends to dislike word limits. I hate feeling confined or restricted, unable to tell the story I want to tell. But it does offer a unique challenge that I enjoy trying to meet.*

The feeling I was trying to recreate in this story was one I used to get a lot while walking home from the bus stop in the dark. We've all been there; hearing noises from the bushes and knowing that it's just the wind or a pet or something, but not being able to shake the feeling that there's something out there. Trying to create that sense in under a hundred words wasn't easy, and being honest, I'm not sure how well I did it. But it was an excuse to revisit the concept of TMWIT *(Christ, that's a terrible acronym, although it is kinda cool that it incorporates my initials. Maybe one to hang onto if I ever go into the tech business), and that's never a bad thing.*

The Girl in the Painting

She sits there. Just as she's always sat there. Perched on the wall, the frame at the slight angle it always comes to rest at, no matter how many times you try to set it straight. Hung above the mantlepiece, a small, ornate clock squatting just beneath it, the face looking out at the room just as hers does. Both faces are round, pale, a little empty as they sit there, watching the people pass in and out of the room and the seasons rotate around the windows.

The frame is ornate, gilded wood, patterns carved into the surface before being delicately accented with gold leaf. A striking border. Or at least, it would have been. Now the gold is beginning to flake and peel a little, scratches and dents, like ugly bruises, marring the surface. Yet despite this, it bears the undying dignity of a wounded soldier, of one that has seen struggles and hardship but will continue to beat on against the tide.

The scene in the picture is a pleasant one. A grassy field, a hill gracefully sloping up in the distance, daisies dotting the green like snowflakes. A deep, green wood rises up towards the side, the trees shrinking as they stretch towards the hill. And in the foreground, there she is. Legs folded beneath her, knees resting on the tartan picnic blanket. A hamper, woven wicker, the lid half raised, the contents shrouded in shade, sits beside her. The sky is a perfect blue, with just the faintest of clouds that accentuate and offset the eggshell emptiness. The sun is out of sight, but its rays can be seen slanting in from behind the painter, dappling the girl's hair and faintly sparkling off the single ring on her finger. It's a simple band of gold, a single white gem set into the metal, matching the twin pieces at her ears.

It's a portrait, really, not a painting. The girl is undisputedly the focus of the piece, and it's easy to see why. You can still remember first buying it, spotting it in a garage sale while you were out of town. Seeing it there, leaned up against a dusty side table, the frame glinting in the sunlight, you wondered how anyone could want to be rid of such a masterpiece. It was the girl who really sold it to you. There was a kind of youthful beauty, an attractive innocence, captured so brilliantly within the brushstrokes that made you certain that you had to have it. The auburn waves of her hair cascading over her shoulders. Her eyes, such a soft green, peering out of the canvas at you. The gentle, graceful slope of her nose, set above a small, half smiling mouth.

But the mouth is no longer smiling.

The eyes are no longer soft.

Even the hair no longer cascades but tumbles and writhes about her neck.

You know now why the lady at the sale was selling it, and why she looked at you with something like pity as you handed over what you thought was a fraction of what its true value must be. A bargain. A good price. A deal.

A deal with the devil.

The price was good.

The cost was terrible.

Looking at it now, you can see him. Standing right behind her, his beard thick and red. Not naturally red, but stained red in patches that have never been washed and will never fade. His shirt, loose and checked, is fluttering about his waist, the sleeves rolled up to the elbows, exposing his tanned, brawny forearms, the dark skin criss-crossed with faint white lines. At his side hangs the axe, the handle a slender wooden limb, the head scratched and dirty.

You'd always wondered why the woman had said the painting was called '*The Coming of the Woodsman*'. Well, now you know. The Woodsman has come. And not just for her.

You saw him on the day you first saw him in the painting. A dark figure, standing at the edge of the forest, almost invisible against the shadows of the trees. An afterthought by the artist, a little detail you'd not noticed before. You thought nothing of it.

Until you saw him in the park that night.

And since then, he's only come closer. Each day, his painted form takes another step towards the girl, her face slowly changing from naively happy to knowingly terrified. And each day, he moves closer to your house. The front of the park. The end of your street. The top of your turning. Until, finally, yesterday, the bottom of your garden.

You don't bother to lock the door. It won't do anything. You know the time has come.

For you, and for the girl in the painting.

The Girl in the Painting

Anyone who knows me knows that I am a big fan of Stephen King. I love him as a writer, and I admire and respect him as a person. Needful Things, *one of his lesser-known books (at least compared to ones like* The Shining *or* IT*), is without doubt my favourite book I've ever read. Seriously, I recommend that book to anyone I meet – including you. If you told me you stopped reading this book at this point so you could go and read* Needful Things, *I would be genuinely thrilled. In my view, there just isn't another writer around today like Stephen King. He is, unquestionably, one of my idols. But enough gushing about him – let's talk about this story.*

The Girl in the Painting *was inspired by a King short story –* The Road Virus Heads North. *After reading that, the concept of a physical manifestation of your own impending doom lodged itself in my brain. I couldn't stop thinking about it. It's the old question: if you could know how long you had left to live, would you want to know? I just wanted to try a new spin on the concept. While King's story is a white-knuckle thrill ride of approaching terror, I wondered what would come from slowing it down somewhat. Less terror, more gradually encroaching dread. I won't say I wanted to paint a picture of slowly creeping doom, because that's too corny even for me, but that was the sort of feeling I wanted to create.*

I will admit that I'm slightly concerned that this was the second story in not-too-distant succession that had a theme of inescapable impending death. Really starting to wonder what past me was going through that made me write stories like this.

What a Date

The date had gone well, as well as a test that someone hadn't revised for and had been expecting to fail but had actually been really easy and had gone very well indeed.

It had started with a lovely picnic in the park, not a car park or a theme park but a proper park-park, with grass and trees and everything. The grass had been cold and a bit damp but that didn't matter, they'd brought a blanket and they spread that on the grass so that their bottoms didn't get cold and damp. He'd said he'd made the sandwiches himself, but that was a lie. He hadn't made the sandwiches himself, as he said he had, because his mother had made them because she was better at making sandwiches and he was busy getting ready and playing on his phone. But the girl didn't know that he hadn't made the sandwiches, as he said he had, because his mother was better at making sandwiches and he was busy getting ready and playing on his phone, because she hadn't been there while his mother was making sandwiches and he was getting ready and playing on his phone.

The sandwiches had been good, because his mother had made them, and afterwards they'd sat on the grass and talked about everything and nothing, although it wasn't really everything because they didn't know everything to talk about everything, and anyway talking about everything would take too long, and it wasn't really nothing because that would mean they didn't talk at all, and they did talk. They talked a lot.

Then they'd gone to her house. It was a nice house, a very nice house, a nicer house than he lived in because he lived in a house that had been cheaper than hers because her family was richer than his and so could afford a house that cost more money and so was nicer. It had a red door. Behind the door was a hallway. They went down the hallway into the kitchen. The kitchen was wide and modern and smelt of food.

It was in the kitchen that they first kissed, his hands on her slender waist; slender because she was thin but not skinny, not so thin that she would look unhealthy or so thin that he would be able to see her ribs when she took her shirt off for him weeks later, but a healthy thin that was pleasant and good looking. The kiss was magical. He enjoyed feeling his lips against hers. Hers tasted sweet, but not too sweet, sweet like syrup but proper syrup like Lyle's syrup, not the cheap supermarket knock-off stuff that's too runny and too sweet because they put too much sugar in it. That sweet.

He didn't think he loved her. It was too early for love. Love comes after years, or at least months, not one date where they ate sandwiches and talked. But maybe, someday, he thought he could love her.

Yeah. Ok. You're probably due an explanation here.

No, I didn't just slap in a piece that I wrote at primary school. Nor was this written by an AI with only vague ideas about human emotion (we prefer to be called Engineered People). No, this was a deliberately awfully written story. During one of my many misspent private study periods during Sixth Form, I found a competition calling for stories that were so bad, they were good. And there was no way I was going to turn down the chance to try something like that. An hour or two later, What a Date *had been written. I showed it to one of my friends, they read it and – direct quote – said, "That is the single worst thing I've ever read. And I've read all the* Twilight *books."*

I think that's all that needs to be said really.

The Cave

Shadows dance against the wall. Flickering, twisting shapes, writhing on the stone, contorting as the flames hesitantly leap, battling the cold air that whistles through the open mouth of the cave. The floor is bare rock, the surface rough and uneven, uncomfortable beneath her back. The fire gives out little heat, the dying flames losing the fight with the frigid breeze. She shivers.

A howl from outside makes her sit up sharply, reaching instinctively for the weapon that lies at her side, never out of reach. She's been attacked while sleeping before, as the scars on her neck – thick, ragged white lines – always remind her. A painful lesson, but an important one.

A snuffling sound.

Something coming close to the mouth of the cave, picking up a scent. A predator? She can't be sure; the light from the fire doesn't dare venture beyond the yawning porthole of darkness. She gets up into a low crouch, blade ready, anticipating the creature's movements even as it makes them.

It hurls itself out of the darkness, a starving, spinning ball of snarling claws and scratching teeth. She catches it, digging her fingers into its hide, feeling rib and bone beneath the thin, ragged fur.

It's a kindness to slide the blade into its throat.

She drops the corpse to the floor, wiping her hands on the walls.

Behind her, he rolls over, small round face pointing towards the roof of the cave, eyes closed and mouth softly gurgling in sleep. Thank goodness he didn't wake up. He'd have attracted every scavenger in the area with his cries. Looking at him, sleeping peacefully, she feels a strange combination of relief and regret.

Things have got to change. They can't go on like this. She'd been fine for years, living in the forests, scavenging the towns if she needed to, quietly dealing with the mutants. She'd been comfortable, happy even, relying only on herself, caring only for herself.

Until she found him, abandoned, alone. Until she swapped her safety for his.

Now she's vulnerable, exposed. Now, she has something she cares about.

Something to lose.

The final lines may be cliché as all hell, but that doesn't stop me liking this story. Again, I tried to keep explanation and context to a minimum. Who the protagonist is, where they are, how they got there, what's attacking them; all that is left ambiguous. Because it doesn't matter to the story. All that matters is that the unnamed woman is alone, in the cave, with a child she's trying to protect. It's a tiny snapshot into a bigger story, and I didn't want it to be anything more than that. Flash fiction should be just that: a flash. A glimpse. A momentary window. And this story is one of the few times I think I've been able to pull that off successfully.

Split

I can't see Him, but I can feel Him.

He's here now. But of course, He's always been here. Just as long as I have.

No-one else can see Him, either. All they see is me. Just me, plain old me, just the one me. They never consider that it might be possible, of course, that far from being one, we may possess two selves. Two people in one body, one physical and one not, one tangible and one untouchable.

He comes with me as I walk down the street, my hands in my jean pockets. The streetlamps are dim and sickly in their yellow light, and I feel like a ghost fading in and out of existence as I drift from pool to pool.

A movement, rounding the corner up ahead.

There! Here it comes! Why else would someone be out at this hour? He's come for you, come to kill you. Look at him, there with his hands at his sides, ready to lunge at you. Big hands, easily able to crush your throat like a paper cup.

No, no, no! He's lying. The figure ahead is no threat to me. It's an older gentleman, shuffling slowly along the pavement, his arms hanging limp from his shoulders. He's probably just been visiting a grandchild, or to the OneStop or something. There's a million reasons for him to be out at this time.

But look at his hands. Big, gnarled hands. Strong hands. They could club you to death easily. And he's still coming at you. You gotta do something before he gets to you!

He's just an old man! He's not going to hurt me! Look, he's not even looking at me.

Because he knows looking at you will draw your attention! It's all part of his plan to relax you, make you ignore him until it's too late and he can pounce at you.

Pounce? Listen to yourself! He doesn't look like he could manage a hop, let alone a pounce. You're being ridiculous. Just shut up, I'll be home soon.

But what if you never make it? What if you never arrive? What if it's because this man with those hands, those big, knotted, strong, twisted hands is going to bundle you into that alleyway there and choke you to death?

He's not! He's not! He's not!

He is! He is! He is and you know he is!

"Excuse me, young man—"

Killer!

Hands close around a throat.

My hands. The man's throat.

The doddery old fool thought he could trick me, lull me into ease so he could finish me off? Pah. The idiot. I saw him for just who he is. Look at him now, his eyes full of panic as he squirms. As if acting innocent is going to save him now.

Good. You're safe now.

His body, limp and empty, falls to the floor. I look down at him, lying there.

And realise, with horror, what He has done.

Split

If you're picking up a lingering waft of Jekyll and Hyde *in this story, then that means I did something right. The competition I wrote this for was being run to celebrate a recent stage adaptation of the book, and they wanted short stories with a similar leaning. I'll admit my take on it isn't exactly faithful to the classic story, but I felt it conveyed a similar sentiment. I will also admit that I shamelessly stole the title from the M. Night Shyamalan thriller with James McAvoy, which is still my favourite film (honestly, the fact that he wasn't even nominated for any major acting awards for that is an absolute joke). So yeah, this story wears its influences on its sleeve. But when its influences are one of most well-regarded works of gothic fiction of all time and a film that contains some of the best acting I've ever seen, is that really a bad thing?*

Dreams

Dreams.

They're funny things, aren't they?

They're not real. We get told this all the time. "It's just a dream." "In your dreams." "Dream on, sunshine." They're made out to be a waste of time, a pointless activity. A fabrication, a fantasy, a pleasant falsehood created to keep our minds busy while we're sleeping or in school.

But dreams can also be powerful.

Martin Luther King Jr had a dream. He made a great speech about it, and look what happened there. One of the most famous oratory performances of all time, a moment that changed a nation. "I have a dream that my four little children will one day live in a nation where they will not be judged by the colour of their skin, but by the content of their character." These words transformed the world we know. All because he had an idea. He had a dream.

ABBA wrote a song about dreams. A beautiful, soft song, about dreams helping people deal with real life; "I have a dream, a fantasy. To help me through reality." So, although dreams aren't real, dreams can impact things that are real. People dream about reaching the top, of making millions, winning gold medals, marrying the one they love. And some of them do these things. They wouldn't do them if they couldn't dream them first.

Shakespeare wrote about dreams. *A Midsummer Night's Dream* blurs the line between dreams and reality. Everyone forgets about the strange events of the night, because they think they were just a dream.

So, are dreams just echoes of the real world? Are dreams just our memories of things we have forgotten? Prospero says in *The Tempest,* "We are such stuff as dreams are made on, and our little life is rounded with a sleep." Does that mean that life is nothing but a dream? Are we nothing more than the products of some great imagination? And if so, what happens when they wake up?

The woman jolted awake, unnerved by the voice in her head. It had been so clear, so real, so not like a dream.

A dream.

That was what it had been talking about.

She almost laughed. She'd been dreaming about dreaming. This was some *Inception* style nonsense right here. Life just being a dream and it ending when someone wakes up.

The boy sleepily opened his eyes, the crusty morning muck momentarily cementing his eyelids together. That was a really weird dream. Some woman, one he didn't know, waking up just as he was. And thinking about dreaming. Just as he was. Weird. What was it she'd wondered? That was it. Whether life was just a dream, and if it ended when someone woke up.

They say that if you can't sleep, it's because you're awake in someone else's dream. They're not quite right. You're not part of someone else's dream. We're all part of something else's dream.

And the alarm clock is slowly, steadily, unstoppably, unavoidably, ticking away.

Christ, how pretentious did I think I was? I remember writing this story, but I have no idea what made me write it. It was supposed to be a Maths cover lesson in Year 12, but for some reason the teacher never showed up. So we basically just pissed around for three-quarters of an hour, and I wrote this. There might have been a competition with the theme of dreams, I'm not sure, but either way.

I feel like I was trying to go for some kind of grand philosophical tone with this, but I'll be honest, I don't think I had the first clue what I was talking about. You know how I know? Because if I were to try and write this again today, four or so years later, I still wouldn't have a clue what I was talking about. This to me feels like something I would try and write to maybe impress someone who was more literary minded than I was, something to make me seem deep and meaningful and well-read. Well, I don't know who I was trying to impress, but it certainly wasn't future me. Future me is looking at this now and cringing hard enough to powderise his bones.

Four Walls

These walls were once white. Clean. Smooth. Four perfect slabs of concrete, carefully and evenly painted. The floor and the ceiling *(lid)* were the same, but only the latter is still clean. The floor is covered in dirt and dust. I won't let Them clean it. The dirt is nice. It's real. It reminds me that not everything is white.

No, not everything is white.

Not these four walls.

They were once white. Not anymore. They were once smooth. So smooth, nice to run a hand over, the cold concrete calming and confining. Confining. Yes. That's what the walls do. They don't comfort. They contain.

The walls are not white anymore.

They are not smooth anymore.

I made them not white. I made them not smooth. I had to.

There is a drawing on the wall by my bunk *(grave)*. No. Not a drawing. A painting. A drawing uses pencils and pens and paper. A painting uses paint and brushes and blood and fingers.

Blood.

Yes. My blood.

They weren't happy about that. They didn't let me eat that day. But that's OK. I don't mind. I prefer not to have to see Them. I like being on my own.

No.

I'm never on my own.

The drawing *(painting. Picture!)* is not very good. I wasn't good at art at school. I couldn't draw the nice things that the other children could. I couldn't mould the pretty faces in clay *(mud)* that they could. But I could do maths. I could do the science. I could work with the computers better than they could. They didn't like that. They didn't like me being better *(superior)* than them. The other kids hurt me. They hurt me. They hurt me.

They can't hurt me now.

That's what They tell me.

But *They* tell me different.

The drawing *(painting)* shows me. I'm good looking, tall, taller than all of the others. I'm at least ten feet tall, so big, so strong. I'm holding a certificate. You can't read the writing, but I know what it is. It's a prize for being the cleverest, the smartest, the bestest. All the other people are clapping because they know I am good and they are not. I can hear them clapping. I can see their faces as they look up to me. I can—

The door opens.

Dr Donegan takes a moment to examine the patient in front of him. Huddled against the wall in his jumpsuit, his eyes far away and unfocused. He's rocking slightly, hugging his knees to his chest. But he doesn't seem to be talking to himself again. That's good. Donegan makes a note of it on his clipboard.

Looking round the cell, he can't see any new marks on the walls. That's good as well. Another scribble, another note taken.

"Hello, Charlie," he says, stepping into the room.

My name is not Charlie.

He's got it wrong. The man has got it wrong. My name is Albert. Why don't They call me Albert?

He comes towards me, carrying the paper he writes on. He won't show me what he writes on the paper. I tried to see once, and They came and hurt me. He looks like he's smiling, like he's my friend. But he won't tell me things. Friends tell each other things. He doesn't tell me things. He's not a friend.

"How are you feeling today, Charlie?" There is no reply. As usual. Donegan sighs, and writes it down, the pen scratching over the surface of the paper. "They told me that you haven't tried to hurt yourself again. That's very good, Charlie."

I'm not Charlie. And I didn't try to hurt myself. They said I did but I didn't. Who are They? He won't tell me who They are. They must be his friends because They tell him things. I've seen people who I think are Them. They come to my room *(prison)* and try to talk to me. Sometimes They hurt me. They are enemies.

He's come into my room *(cell)*. He's tried to talk to me.

He's one of Them.

I can't talk to him. I can't go near him. He's one of Them and They are enemies and enemies are dangerous and try and hurt you like the kids at school.

I put my head on my knees. If I don't look at him he'll go away. He'll go away and leave me on my own.

No.

Not on my own.

Donegan looks at the man a little longer, then shakes his head.

"Charlie, I want to show you something." He goes over to the rocking man, squats down beside him. There's a photograph in his pocket, an old-fashioned polaroid, crinkled and folded. He pulls it out and holds it out to the man. "Charlie? Charlie. Look at this."

One eye peers over the top of the knee, filled with fear.

"Do you know who this is, Charlie?"

There's no answer. Nothing but terror in the single eye, which stares at him for a second, then disappears back into the knee. Donegan sighs, stands, turns and, writing as he goes, walks out of the door.

There's a woman waiting outside. Dark skin and hair, a pristine white lab coat, and very thick glasses. She's sucking a peppermint, rolling the sweet around her mouth as Donegan leaves the room.

"Any change?" she asks.

Donegan shakes his head. "Just the same. How long has he been in there?"

"Nearly a year now. Did he react to the photo?"

"No. Looked right through it."

"Think we'll ever be able to let him out?"

I know who was in the photo.

It was me. And Elsie.

I don't know who Elsie is *(was. Was?)*. Yes. She *was*.

I don't know who Elsie was.

She's why you're here.

I don't know what *They* mean. Elsie *(bitch)* is a name I know but I don't know why I know.

You do know who she is.

No, I don't know who she is. I don't know what *They* mean.

I look over at the other walls. These don't have drawings *(paintings)* on them. They have carvings *(gougings)* on them. I stole a knife from my food. They didn't like that. They hurt me for that. But it was OK. I did the carvings.

They tried to tell me what the carvings were. They don't know what they are. I know because I'm clever and I did them. They are stupid. They can't see what they are.

I can hear voices outside. Talking.

Talking about me.

I know it. I know They are talking about me. What if They're planning to come and hurt me? They've hurt me before. They can do it again. What if this time They don't stop with hurting? What if They know about *Them*? How *They* have been talking to me, telling me what They're doing, about why I'm really here.

Why am I here?

Elsie.

The walls are moving.

They're coming in, pressing in, coming closer and closer to me.

I can't get out. I can't go anywhere.

I can never get out.

They're going to kill me.

The walls are not white. They're dirty *(real)* and covered in carvings and drawings (*paintings)* that I did because I had to because *They* told me to and *They* know things and *They* tell me things and *They* are my friends and *They* will help me escape (*kill)* from Them.

I can't escape from Them.

The walls are crushing me. I can't breathe. I can't get away. I push against them but they're too strong. They're killing me, pressing against me, squashing me, breaking me, destroying me.

I scream.

I can't stop screaming.

*

They came for me.

They came bursting through my door into my room *(prison)* and grabbed me and threw me on my bed and held me down and gave me drugs *(poison)* and left me here. Still screaming.

I've stopped screaming now.

Because I'm thinking.

Why am I here?

Elsie.

Who is Elsie?

Bitch.

Why is she a bitch?

She put you here.

Why?

Bitch.

They aren't telling me things any more.

Have *They* turned against me too?

No. Please no. *They* can't leave me. *They*'re all I have.

They want to kill me. *They* want to kill me, and They want to kill me.

I'm going to die here. I'm going to die here in this room *(cell)* and no one will ever know because nobody knows who I am and I don't know why I'm here *(Elsie)* and I'll never get out because They want me here and *They* want me dead and—

I hit my head against the wall. Hard.

It hurts. But that is good.

I do it again. And again. And again.

Finally, when the room is blurry and the white wall running with red, I stop.

I feel better.

Why am I here?

"Doctor Donegan. Tell me, how is Patient 079?"

Donegan shifts uncomfortably in his seat. "There's been little change, sir," he says, carefully measuring out each word. "He gave no reaction to the photo of him and Miss Greywater. He doesn't appear to have self-harmed again, nor does it seem that he's made any more illustrations on the walls."

"That sounds like progress to me, Doctor. Sounds like he's over the hump and moving into the next phase."

"I'm not so sure, sir. You remember what 079 was like before we locked him up?"

"Of course, Doctor. You know I take an interest in all our patients."

"Patient 079 was one of our most challenging, and most damaging cases, sir. He was intelligent, rational and patient. While he is certainly not like he was anymore, I think he may be attempting to deceive us as to his state."

"Why would he want to do that?"

"I don't know, sir. But there was just ..." Donegan trails off. "Something didn't feel right. I think we need to watch him very carefully. We don't want him killing anyone else."

They haven't said anything else, but I can feel *Them* there. Waiting. But I'm ignoring *Them*. Because I need to think.

If Elsie *(bitch)* is the reason I'm here, as *They* say, then Elsie *(bitch)* must have done something, or I did something with Elsie (*bitch!)*

Stop calling her a bitch!

Not her.

What do you mean?

Not her.

She's not a bitch? Then why do you keep calling her one?

Not her.

Why won't you tell me what happened?

Photo.

Photo? The one the man had? But he's one of Them. He can't help me.

Photo.

OK. The photo. It was me and Elsie – Don't say it!

We were ... in a park. On grass; green grass. There was a tree behind us.

That wasn't in the picture.

How do I know that?

Sunlight through the leaves. Cars passing on a road. Coffee in the air. A faint yapping. And a voice. My voice.

"Is it a boy or—?"

A soft voice. A woman's voice. Elsie's voice.

"No. She's a bitch."

Bitch.

Bitch.

Bitch!

Bitch! Bitch! Bitch! Bitch!

I remember.

I remember everything.

"Sir, as you know, we were pioneering a new technique when Patient 079 was brought to us. Before, it was simply a case of keeping our patients in solitary on a permanent basis, so that they could do no more damage. But as more and more people were brought to us, we realised we were going to be unable to contain them all. There were just too many. So, we moved away from containment, towards what could be called a 'cure' for our problem. Patient 079 was the ninth patient that we tried this new procedure on."

"The procedure being to lock him in a soundproofed room and leave him there."

"Yes, sir. After the psychoactive agents had been administered, we moved Patient 079 to one of our experimental facilities."

"And it worked, didn't it? Just like it did on the others?

"I'm afraid I don't think so, sir." Donegan took a deep breath. "With the previous eight patients, it took no longer than seven months for them to completely lose their minds. You've seen the effect the procedure had on them. It was even more impressive than we were expecting."

"I'll say. They were barely human anymore. Sheer rambling idiots. Once they'd gotten over the madness and self-harming stage, they were just husks. Empty shells. Nobody would listen to a word they said, even if they could remember what they knew. We just packed them off to psychiatric units, problems solved. Are you saying 079 is different?"

"I fear so, sir."

"What symptoms is he showing?"

"We've found characteristics of amnesia, paranoia, schizophrenia, just about everything you'd expect after being locked in a noiseless box for weeks. But, sir, he's been in that room nearly twelve months now. It is certainly true; his mental condition has deteriorated severely. His intellect is a shadow of its former self. He may not even remember why he's here. But he's still functional. He's still, at least somewhat, rational. I fear that he's too dangerous to ever be released back into any kind of normal mental health facility. But we can't keep him here, sir."

"Why not, Donegan?"

"Every day he stays here, every day he sees me, sees one of the guards, sees the corridor outside his room, he learns a little bit more about where he is. Anything, the smallest detail, could be enough to trigger a mental recall. He's unstable, definitely. But not broken. He's like a car balanced exactly on a cliff edge, sir. He's so very close to falling. But the balance is so fine, all he needs is a breath of wind to push him back onto solid ground."

"Are you saying that we need to terminate the experiment?"

Donegan nodded. "I'm as disappointed as you are, sir. This will be *Clinico's* first failure in years. But yes, I think it is unavoidable."

"Very well. I'll dispatch the clean-up crew at once."

Elsie wasn't a bitch.

She was my girlfriend. A chemist, a brilliant scientist. Beautiful. Kind. Funny. So, so clever.

And so good at lying.

It was an accident, really. I didn't mean to. I was just looking for a pen, mine had broken. I know she'd said to never go in her study, but it was only a pen. I was just looking for a pen.

Instead, I found a nightmare.

The pictures.

The horrible pictures.

The bodies. The burns. The blisters.

Her company name, *Clinico*, in the corner of every photo, at the top of every page.

She was a killer. I was living with a killer.

That was when she came in.

I can't remember clearly what happened.

I remember her shouting; me cowering.

The gun firing.

She'd pulled it out. I don't know from where. I'd never seen a gun before. Never wanted to. Hate guns. Especially now.

I really didn't mean to.

She was going to shoot me. I remember falling, struggling, wrestling.

The gun firing.

Blood.

Blood everywhere.

Blood on my face. Blood on my hands. Blood on the carpet. Blood in her hair.

They came for me after that.

They came for me and pumped me full of drugs and threw me in this room and left me to rot.

Because I know who They are. I know what They do.

They broke me. But *They* fixed me.

No. Not *They*. I am *They*. *They* are me.

I get to my feet. My forehead is still bruised and bleeding where I hit it against the wall. But that doesn't matter. I can barely feel it.

Memories are swirling around my head like bubbles round a plughole. Random flashes of colour, whispered words, snatches of smells. My whole head is spinning.

And the walls are pressing in again.

I can't escape. I can't leave. I'm better but that just means They'll keep me here forever because now I really know what They're doing. They made me forget but now I know and if They know I know then They'll give me more drugs and lock me in here again and maybe They'll kill me because I know Them and They know me and I can expose Them and They don't want me to expose Them so They'll kill me so I can't expose Them and I'm going to die here in this room I'm going to die and the walls are coming in and I can't breathe and can't leave and can't escape and can't live.

I don't even know I'm at the door until I'm pummelling with my fists, beating it like the drums I used to play (how could I forget the drums? Spent all my time playing the drums. Loved the drums. So did Elsie. I got good at the drums) for Elsie. I hit at the metal again and again and again but it doesn't do anything except hurt my hands. But I hold onto the pain. The pain is real. Real, like the dirt on the walls and floor.

The walls are closing in. Faster and faster. They're screaming towards me, dirty and real, coming to crush me, to kill me, to end me, to silence me.

The door opens.

It slides open so suddenly that both me and the man behind it just stand for a moment in shock, neither expecting to see the other there. He's tall, broad, thickset, in a black uniform. And he has a gun.

That breaks the spell for me.

I hate guns.

I shove the man with as much force as my weak and wasted muscles can muster. I never was very strong, but desperation and fear fuel my actions. The man is caught completely off guard. He flails, loses his balance, and falls backwards, his head smacking against the concrete wall of the passageway behind him. I hear shouting from behind him, and am ready when the next guard swings into the doorway, his gun in both hands, looking for me. Seeing me too late.

I bring my bare foot swinging up between his legs, catching him directly in the groin with the knuckles of my toes. Pain crunches through my foot, but it's nothing compared to what the guard feels, I'm sure. Good. Bastard deserved it for pointing a gun at me. He crumples over, the gun clattering to the floor, his face radish-red. I grab him by the shoulders and hurl him sideways, past the door and into his waiting colleagues. I don't think I've done enough to hurt any of them, but it's given me a window.

I have to get out. I can't die here in this cell.

I stumble out of the doorway. My legs aren't used to running. It's been nearly a year since I did any exercise, and my limbs move in an awkward, ungainly way. But I'm desperate. I don't want to die.

I run, or try to run, as fast as I can. Cell doors, each one identical to mine, flash past, white rectangles in grey concrete, each one running towards my pursuers as I flee from them. My feet slap on the floor with each step, the sounds ringing in my ears and along the passageway.

I can't see the end.

The passageway goes on forever.

I can't leave it.

It goes on and on and on and on and on and on and on and on and on and on and on and on and on, a never-ending cuboid of grey punctuated by white rectangles that is infinite.

I can't escape.

The guards are going to catch me any second. I can run and run and run and run and run but any second I'm going to hear a gunshot and I'm going to fall over and I'm going to die and They will take my body away and They will destroy it and They will make sure nobody ever knows what happened because They are everywhere and I am nothing and I'm going to die I'm going to die I'm—

I run straight into the door at the end of the corridor.

It appeared out of nowhere, so solid and real that I almost knock myself out on the hard metal surface. The breath is driven from my lungs, and I momentarily see stars. But when my vision clears, it is most definitely a door. A way out that has, like magic, appeared in the endless corridor.

It's locked.

I wrench at that handle, screaming because I know the guards are coming and that I'll be dead soon and that there's nothing I can do. I wonder why I haven't taken a bullet in the back already. Maybe They are just toying with me because they know I have nowhere to go.

A fire alarm.

It's there, beside the door, with the instructions screaming out to me in white letters. I pummel the glass and frantically search for the button beneath.

The ensuing wail lets me know I've succeeded.

The alarm is deafening, an unbearable screech made all the worse by my months of silence. I'm almost certain my ears are bleeding. Pain fills my entire head. Images of Elsie. The gunshot. My crying. The blood on the carpet.

The fire extinguisher is very heavy. I don't even know I'm holding it until I've wrenched out the pin and am spraying thick white gas into the air. The guards had been advancing down the corridor, but suddenly are greeted by a wall of choking white vapour. The overhead sprinklers automatically kicked in when the alarm was triggered, and suddenly the passageway is filled with water and smoke. I keep spraying, desperate to keep them back. I hear them stumbling and slipping, swearing and spluttering.

The extinguisher is empty.

I throw it as hard as I can at head height, and hear a sickening thud, immediately followed by a short, sharp scream that cuts off almost as soon as it begins. Or maybe it's just the alarm drowning out all sound. A gun goes off, louder even than the siren, and Elsie's face, her beautiful face, blood on her chin and in her hair, flashes before me. A few drops of blood, real blood, splatter the wall just outside the white cloud. Seeing it brings on a wave of dizziness and nausea, sending the passageway spinning around me. The blood on the carpet. The blood on the carpet. The blood on the carpet.

I slap myself in the face. Hard. And things stop spinning.

Maybe I can get past them. If I make a run for it now, before the steam has fully dissipated, maybe I can escape.

The door opens.

The man who came into my cell is standing in the doorway. His mouth is open in disbelief, his eyes wide with shock. He still holds that bloody clipboard that he used to keep his notes about me on.

Dr Donegan can't quite believe what is before his very eyes.

Patient 079 is stood in the doorway of the Silent Wing, his eyes bloodshot and wild, his jumpsuit damp and baggy. Blood drips from a dark wound on his forehead, the red mixing with the dark hair and matting it to his brow. The corridor behind him is filled with white gas, and the fire control system is pouring down from the ceiling. There's a fresh blood spray on the wall, and the ear-splitting siren, bouncing off the walls of the narrow space, continues to scream.

But Donegan barely registers any of this.

It's the eyes. The eyes of Patient 079.

Gone is the blank dullness, the empty incomprehension. The fear, the paranoia, is still there. He doesn't need his decade of psychological training and experience to see that. That is plain as day.

But there is a cold understanding there, a burning fury. The eyes are like an icy vice, and Donegan can almost feel the smouldering fires of hatred burning behind them.

"Charles," he begins. "Charles, I—"

I headbutt him right in the open mouth.

It's a mistake.

I was aiming for his nose, Glaswegian style, but he pulls back at the last second. His front teeth, beautifully straight and white as can be, meet my bruised and bloody forehead. And sink right into it.

Both of us scream. Or he tries to. My head is in the way.

I wrench myself backwards, out of his mouth. Two teeth, an incisor and a canine, come with me, buried in the skin of my forehead, just above my eyebrows. The pain is blinding. More fresh rivulets of blood run over my face. The man with the clipboard staggers, blood dripping from his mouth. I shove him aside. I can see daylight behind him, can smell fresh, non-machined air drifting in through the door.

Freedom.

The passageway opens into a wide, open space. I can feel a breeze on my face for the first time in months, can hear sounds other than my own maddening heartbeat, see with light that's not artificial.

The sun.

How I have missed you.

Even though I know that every moment I stand here is another moment I could take a bullet between the shoulder blades, I just have to stand for a second, drinking it all in.

For the first time in a year, I'm glad to be alive. I feel something I thought I'd lost forever.

Hope.

It's short lived.

I'm still trapped.

The outdoor space is a yard. Flat, featureless and empty. There are a few outbuildings on the other side, and beyond them ...

A wall.

Behind me: a wall.

Four Walls

To both sides: two more dirty, bloody, heartless walls.

I can't escape.

Fate really is a bitch.

She led me on the merry song and dance, gave me back my mind, made me feel like I had a chance. And now?

I'm back where I started.

Trapped by four walls.

Four Walls

This story was another product of me watching Split *for the first time and falling completely in love with it.*

Now, as I said in my prelude to this collection, I'm all but certain that this does not ring even close to true as a portrayal of any kind of mental illness. It should not be taken as such. I just got fixated on the idea of someone being trapped within their own head, making their own mind a prison for them, stuck within their own mental walls. And that then developed into wondering if someone could be trapped there against their will, maybe by someone else for some nefarious purpose.

Could someone artificially induce some form of psychosis in someone else as a way to keep them quiet? Why not? I'll admit that this was a development that occurred to me some ways into writing this, and so the story may not fully track with this remit in mind. I was in something of a rush to get this one finished, as I recall, so I don't think I had much time to edit and tweak it to better fit with the new concept. Regardless, I still like this piece. I'm not going to say how it could or should be read, or what messages I wanted readers to take away from it. All I'll say is thank you to my editor, Nic, because the formatting for this story must have been an absolute bitch.

Damsel in Distress

Damsel in distress. Wanting ripped superhero to come sweep me off my feet and fly me around the world for passionate times. Jazz lover. Mail 54873.

That was how the ad went, and I have to admit, it made me chuckle. Although most women will challenge the stereotype that all they desire is a strong, chiselled man with biceps like basketballs, now and then you do come across one who not only embraces said stereotype but throws herself headlong into it. 'Ripped superhero'. I only had to read those words for Bonnie Tyler's eighties' hit to start dancing through my head. Does this woman think superhumans like that actually exist? I don't mean insanely shredded dudes. They exist. God knows they exist. Everybody knows they exist because they won't stop posting photos of themselves all over the damn internet. We get it, you spend a lot of time in the gym. You've got thighs bigger than my head. Whoop-de-do for you.

(On a side note, having that much testosterone racing through your body is known to have some unfortunate side effects. Side effects like, for example, genital shrinkage. So who're the real winners here? Average dudes for the win!)

But having big arms doesn't make you a superhero. Not in the traditional sense anyway. I guarantee you that this woman (who I'll call Dina the Dreamer from now on, for no reason) wants a man who's loyal, brave, caring, giving and charming. The kind of senselessly and inexplicably altruistic character created by a young child making up their first playtime superhero. Most guys can manage two or three of the above qualities. Four at a push. So, if Dina really thinks she's gonna find someone who's all five, plus is built like a brick wall and who doesn't have a ding-dong you could use as a replacement ball in ping-pong, she's either stupid or high. Maybe both.

Oh, and he's gotta be rich, too. Can't forget that. How else could he 'fly' Dina around the world for those passionate times? Passionate too. Means he's got to be a good lover on top of everything else. Not just virile, but compassionate, tender, loving. The kind of guy who'd go down on her and not ask for any reciprocation. She really is out of her mind if she thinks people like that exist outside of her fantasies.

So, let's review. Dina is looking for a travel-loving, well-off, passionate lover, with abs you could scrub your laundry on, enough love to answer the Black Eyed Peas (look up the album *Elephunk* if that went over your head), and who somehow isn't a figment of a lonely female imagination stirred up by reading too many cheap romance novels while downing boxes of red wine.

Oh, and he has to be well hung too.

That's the kind of man she's looking for.

I take a marker, and put a circle around the ad.

Why the hell not?

Damsel in Distress

A somewhat tongue-in-cheek entry, Damsel in Distress *was a writing exercise we were given in one of my university creative writing seminars. My professor thought it would be funny to show us a bunch of ads from when people actually had to use newspapers to put themselves out there, and then ask us to write a piece that incorporated them in some way. After reading some of the ads, I was kinda surprised at the way some of them were worded. So I decided to write the sort of sarcastic response that a put-upon beta male might write after being rejected one too many times. Let's not dwell on where I might have gotten my inspiration from. And then, just because I'd given up on this piece ever being taken seriously, I had to add him deciding to respond to the ad. Why the hell not?*

Dustbowl Daphne (Giddy-Up My Heart)

Our tale begins with a tumbleweed, as so many of these tales do. A tumbleweed that bounced and rolled slowly across the dusty street, as tumbleweeds on the streets of these western towns are known to do. Carried along by the breeze that stirred up the dirt, it drifted aimlessly around the town before finally coming to rest at the hooves of a chestnut stallion. The horse was tethered to a wooden rail outside the old saloon that stood at the edge of the town, put there to be the first place any visitor would come across. And visitors there had been aplenty lately.

There were two more horses tied up alongside Nutmeg Nag that day. The three belonged to Barnaby Spades, aka Buckshot Barney, Sammy Hindle, sometimes called Shotgun Sam, and Abe Crowshaw, better known as Crimson Crowshaw after his bloodstained bandanna and Stetson. Despite his nickname and reputation, the garments weren't stained with the blood of fallen foes. A pig had jumped him while he was trying to rustle some nearby steers. Abe pulled his gun in fright and shot that sow between the eyes. That's where his infamous fashion pieces came from.

Those three were a group of local rustlers who'd managed to just about stay on the right side of the law. They weren't exactly chummy with the sheriff, but they could at least wander into town for a drink and not be chased right back out again. That's exactly what they'd been doing on that afternoon, knocking down beers and complaining about the circus being in town. That was the reason there'd been so many folks wandering the streets of that little town. Buffalo Bill's Wild

West Show was in town, and folks were coming from all over to see it. But those three weren't happy about all the strangers wandering the streets. Made it too hard to wrangle any cattle.

The three of them came out of the bar and looked out towards the huge canvas construction that had been put up just outside town for the event. There'd been parades and staged shootouts, horse racing and sharpshooting, animal shows and animal hunts. It was the last day before it moved on, and the three cowboys would be glad to be rid of it.

As the three of them stood beside their steeds, preparing to mount up and ride off into the sunset like cowboys are supposed to do, Shotgun Sam grabbed Crowshaw by the arm and gestured towards the entrance booth that stood at the end of the street, as if hoping anyone walking through town would be funnelled right into it.

"Here, Abe, looky there," he drawled, eyes wide and shining.

"Le'go of my arm," Crowshaw grumbled, shaking his partner off. "What's matter?"

"Look at that there ticket booth. Notice anything?"

Crowshaw looked towards the little striped tent that stood before the much larger white tent, but couldn't see anything unusual. It was red and white, with a little window cut into the fabric, and what looked like a real horseshoe hung above the opening, nailed to a plank of wood.

"What—?" he began, then stopped as his eyes focused suddenly. Not on the booth, but the person inside it.

"It's a dame," Buckshot Barney mused, staring in the same direction. "What's a dame doing there? Ain't that a man's job? Dealing with folks and the like. All a man would have to do is raise his voice at her and she'd let him in free."

"Naw man, I think you're being too harsh on the womenfolk," Crowshaw said. "I reckon she could do the job well as any of us. Just taking money and giving tickets ain't it?

"Besides," he grinned, "long as she's sitting out there in front of us, I'm not gonna complain about it."

"With you on that one, Abe," chuckled Sam, who was having to make an effort not to let his jaw flop open as his mind worked on other matters.

Their opportunistic ogling session was interrupted by the clack of hooves coming down the street towards them. The three rustlers turned and froze.

A black shape was making its way through the town, silhouetted against the afternoon sun. The marks that its hooves left in the dust were the size of tea saucers, and its shadow darkened the ground a good nine or ten feet in front of it. Crowshaw, who was by nobody's standards a small man, would struggle to get his hat to reach the horse's shoulder. But if the horse was huge, the man sat astride it was monstrous. He loomed high above its pointed head, one fist, the size of a pumpkin, mussing the jet-black mane. If he and the horse had been on level footing, he could have stared it in the eye without even having to look up. As he drew near, the three men could make out four revolvers brazenly displayed on his person. The two worn at his hips were a cowboy standard, but it was the additional two hanging under his arms that drew the attention, as the polished metal flashed in the sun. Two leather straps wrapped around his chest, each one brimming with bullets.

"That ain't—"

"It is."

"It can't be, Abe. There's no way—"

"Black Jack Bowers."

Everyone knew the name Black Jack Bowers. Not many know his backstory though, only his reputation. But sometimes that's all a man needs. Black Jack Bowers started off as a poker hustler, which was where his nickname came from. Doesn't matter who he was playing against, he'd win the shirt right off their back, and no one would have a clue how he did it. Then, one day, he won big against a nasty piece of work called Larry The Legless (after his intolerance for drink). Larry wasn't too happy about that, so he and his gang started a fight with Black Jack. There were six men in that gang. Not one of them walked out alive.

Since then, Jack'd been all over the place. Rustling, wrangling, robbing, whatever. He had more deaths on his hands than he did bullets in his bandoleers. Sheriff wouldn't touch him; he didn't dare. Black Jack Bowers wasn't just big, he was smart too. He knew a lot about a lot of people. Their friends, families, whatever. No one dared cross him.

Jack rode on up towards the three cowboys, and it was then that Crowshaw noticed that his horse was limping on its right foreleg. He could tell straight away that it needed a new shoe, just by the way it was gingerly putting its hoof down. His daddy had owned a ranch and a fair few horses of his own, and he'd learned to read the little signals the magnificent beasts gave off. Jack drew up outside the blacksmith that was stood next to the saloon, noticed with annoyance that the shop was closed and empty, then turned his gaze on the three quivering cowboys.

"Where's Duncan?" he growled at them.

"He's gone to take in the show," answered Abe, trying to keep his voice steady. "Won't be back for another few hours."

Jack Bowers face darkened. "Y'all know anything 'bout shoeing horses? Hercules here lost hers while making a getaway yesterday." He patted his horse on the side of the neck.

Barney, the only one of the three who'd ever read a book in his life, opened his mouth to comment that the Greek hero Hercules had definitely been a male, before being silenced by Shotgun Sam slapping a palm across his mouth.

"I could, you know, take a look at it," swallowed Crowshaw. "I'd need a shoe though. Don't have any spares."

Jack glowered again, before squinting as something caught the light from the slowly sinking sun and bounced it into his eye. The other three turned to see what had caused it, and gulped in unison. It was the horseshoe stuck above the window of the ticket booth. The female occupant was nowhere to be seen, which came as some relief at least.

Without a word, Jack dismounted from his horse, his huge leather boots pluming up the dust as they hit the ground, and strode over towards the empty tent, his spurs jangling musically as he went. The three watched with bated breath as he reached the fabric structure, leaned up, and tore the wooden plank free. Without stopping, he grasped the horseshoe in one hand, the plank in the other, and very smoothly pulled one free of the other. He didn't even look like he was trying.

From their position outside the saloon, Crowshaw and his friends were close enough to witness what came next.

"Hey! What're you doing?"

Black Jack Bowers, face like thunder in preparation for a confrontation, spun around to face the source of the voice.

And froze solid.

The woman from the ticket booth was standing, hands on her hips, looking defiantly up into the huge man's face. In contrast to the three rustlers, who'd nearly needed new pants after seeing Jack ride up, she didn't seem in the least bit frightened.

Abe had started forward, certain that he was going to have to try and intervene before Buffalo Bill needed to find a new ticket seller. But he'd only taken two steps before pausing, and watching the scene unfold. Instead of immediately drawing one of his guns, Jack had remained motionless, staring down at the woman before him.

"I ..." He tried to speak, but his words seemed to be failing him. He glanced down at his hands, which were still clutching the recently separated plank and horseshoe. "My ... Um ... My horse ..." He gestured vaguely in the direction in which Hercules still stood.

The woman looked down at what he was holding, looked back up at his face, and then burst out laughing. Crowshaw, who'd never so much as heard of anyone even talking back to Black Jack Bowers, was now watching some laugh directly into his face. He started moving again, sure that Jack must be about to tear the woman's head off with his bare hands. But still the big man didn't move, merely kicking his heels as he took a pointed interest in his leather boots.

"Come with me, darling," the woman giggled, taking his arm. "We got a whole bunch of spare shoes round the back, you only had to ask." Jack, whose face had now gone so red it was almost purple, could only stammer unintelligibly as she led him towards the entrance. "What do they call you, big guy?"

Abe turned back to his two companions, jaw so slack it was almost resting on the top of his sternum.

"Did you guys see that?"

"Sure did!" Breathed Sam. "The ankles on that girl ..." He gave a low whistle. Abe clipped him across the shoulder.

"Not that. The way she dealt with Jack. Ain't never seen nobody talk to him like that. And the way he acted! What did we just witness?"

"I don't know, Abe," said Barney slowly. "But I got the feeling this story is only just beginning."

Dustbowl Daphne (Giddy-Up My Heart)

I couldn't decide which title to give this story, so I decided to slap both of them on and call it a day. This was a product of a competition that gave its participants three things: a genre, a setting, and an item. Each one was randomly chosen from a list of hundreds, and we were just told to make something up from there. What did I get? Rom-Com, The Old West, and a horseshoe. And just like that, I was away. I really was lucky that the setting and the item matched up so well – God knows how I'd have managed to fit a horseshoe into a sci-fi setting.

I'll be the first to admit, romance is not something that comes particularly naturally to me when I'm writing (or in general, if I'm being honest). So, mindful as ever of my word count, I decided to try and describe the commencement of a romance, rather than its development or conclusion. That left the comedy bit – something else that, as my friends can tell you, I struggle with. So yeah, it's a little cliched; the big cowboy that everyone's afraid of getting flustered and nervous at the sight of a pretty woman. But hey, I did my best. This may not be one of my best stories, but I enjoyed writing something different for a change.

Isolation

Seventeen days.

Seventeen days I've been stuck inside.

Or is it eighteen? I can't even remember. Time has lost all meaning to me. One day blurs into another and another and another like the carriages of a racing train.

I've watched and rewatched every film and TV program that interests me. I've done more reading than I did in my entire life before this, and been on so many daily runs that the soles of my shoes are starting to wear through. I've reorganised my room three times, and each time it's ended up pretty similar to how it started.

My sister won't leave her room, always on the phone to her friends. The idiots keep talking about breaking the rules, going out to drink or shag or whatever. Don't they understand that we got here because of people like them who didn't follow the advice? And now we've gone from advice to guidelines to laws, and they still flout them. And then they have the gall to complain about this when they're prolonging it?

Then again, I can hardly criticise.

Mum's worried about work. The people on the telly keep talking about how people don't need to panic, that they'll take care of it and keep everyone paid, but it's just talk, talk, talk. Words, words, words. At least she's keeping to the rules, though. Shopping trip once a week. Staying indoors as much as possible, only going out with the dog. She's sensible. She's keeping us safe.

And then I screwed it up.

Isolation

Can you blame me? I was going mad, cooped up in here day after day after day, listening to the noises politicians make to try and reassure people. And there she was, also bored out of her mind, just five minutes' walk away and with a surplus of alcohol. How could I say no? And I'll admit, that night was exactly what I needed.

Until I started coughing.

Still, it probably doesn't mean anything.

I mean, it's just a little cough.

It doesn't mean I'm sick.

Right?

Right?

Isolation

No guesses where this one came from. Before any of you ask, no, this was not based on a real-life happening. Sorry to disappoint all of you who love juicy gossip and drama, but I didn't sneak out and hook-up with someone during lockdown. I was actually seeing someone at the time. No, this was just a story that occurred to me during those days of isolation. I knew that people were doing stuff like this, and it annoyed me, and I wanted to express that. I was also annoyed by people's unwillingness to face reality. It calls to mind a line from the fourth series of Blackadder: "If nothing else works, then a total pig-headed unwillingness to look facts in the face will see us through."

The way people had been denying how much of a problem this was had been annoying me for a while, so I decided to push it one step further, and ask this: would these people still pretend it wasn't an issue if they themselves got sick? In my head? Yeah, I think they would. And that also annoyed me. That's about all there is to say really.

Rip and Tear

(Warning: Graphic Violence)

I taste blood in my mouth.

So I'm still alive. That's a nice surprise.

The room I'm in is small; no windows, a single door. The walls and floor are made of the same smooth, cold cobblestones, the polished surfaces a uniform grey. As I stand, the door before me opens, swinging silently aside. Beyond is a passageway, the same grey stones lining its entire length. I leave the cell slowly, the thick soles of my boots creating ringing footfalls as I move.

The passage is well lit, but not from any visible source. The very air itself seems to glow. The ceiling, only a few feet above my head, is bare. No bulbs hang from it, no torches adorn the walls. I care little for these details. Being able to see is enough.

Another door waits at the end of the passage, this one of polished metal. As I approach this one, it too opens, revealing a much larger room beyond. It opens out into a wide circle, the cobbled floor flat and uninterrupted by furniture. As I enter, multiple other doors around the circumference of the room open, showing more passages behind them. Figures step out of the doorways, some tentative, others bold. They glance around, taking in their surroundings, then each other. None of them know what to make of our current situation.

A voice, low and deep, speaks from nowhere, the single word echoing around the room.

"Fight."

The two dozen other people in the room seem to need no incentive. As soon as the word is spoken, they charge at each other, some yelling in rage, some furiously silent. They fall upon each other, clawing at eyes, tearing at throats, stomping and scratching, bites and blows raining down upon flesh as the blood begins to rain down upon the floor.

I stand and watch them, unmoving.

The weak are easily weeded out. Within two minutes, at least fifteen lie dead on the floor, bones broken and organs pulverised. Blood gathers in the seams of the cobblestones. The survivors back away from each other, taking stock, catching their breath, bloodshot eyes filled with bloodlust staring out from beneath bloody brows.

And then they notice me. Still standing. Still waiting.

A thickly built woman to my right comes at me first. She adopts the same attitude as before, running full speed at me, strings of flesh hanging from her nails as they reach for my face. She's five metres from me. Three metres. Two.

Just as her outstretched fingers breach my personal space, I neatly step aside, reaching out with my own right hand as I do so. My thick fingers close around her forearm, clamping down on the flesh. Her screams of anger rise an octave as they become screams of pain, the bones in her arm cracking beneath my grip. I pull her around and slam her onto the ground, her face impacting the stones with a soft crunch. This is immediately followed by a much louder crunch, as my foot descends savagely onto the back of her head. The woman's skull offers only token resistance, before giving way and exploding beneath my heel. Blood, bone, and brain matter splatter across the ground.

The other combatants are still stood where they had backed off to. Not one of them has moved. They are not shocked by the violence; some of them committed much more brutal acts on the bodies that are slowly draining in the centre of the room. Nor are they scared, of me or each other. They are contemplating, calculating, considering. They look at each other, then at me, then at each other.

And then, they attack again.

It's amazing how a common threat can bring people together. These ten or so remaining survivors were the most mortal enemies mere seconds ago, willing to kill each other in a heartbeat. Now, they attack me together, not rushing in, not hurrying, but moving with an instinctive co-ordination. They are like cavemen, unintelligent but able to act on inbuilt urges to work together to take down the tiger.

Now, it is my turn to run. I charge at the nearest one, a slight man with pale skin. He sees me coming, and nimbly dodges aside, trying to swing a punch and catch me on the back of my head as I pass. He, however, is far too slow.

My feet slide on the cobbles as I turn and stop, my leg extending behind me as I lunge into the brake. I use my lowered position to tackle the skinny man to the floor, his head rebounding as it smacks into the stones. I seize his wrist with both hands, plant a foot on his chest, and pull.

His arm tears free from its socket with a wet ripping sound, the flesh stretching and separating in strings. He screams, staring at his now empty shoulder, the wound streaming blood in a viscous torrent. I swing the arm like a club, the protruding knob of bone impacting the side of my next attacker's head. The blow does little more than daze him, but it grants me time to drop the arm, grab his head with both hands, and slam it down, bringing my knee sharply up at the same moment. His fragile facial bones connect with the rigid mass of my patella, and they instantly shatter, the fragments driven up into his brain by the force. He is dead before he can even hit the floor.

Six more opponents face me; two male, four female. They're spread in a half circle before me, trying to stay out of reach as they internally debate their next move.

I make the decision for them, moving towards the woman on my left. She bares her teeth at me in an animalistic rage, her bloodstained lips parting in a hideous smile. As soon as the gap between us begins to close, she leaps at me like a monkey, arms and legs raised as she flies through the air. I raise my right arm in defence, and she latches onto me, her legs wrapping around my waist. She sinks her teeth into the flesh of my arm, manic glee alight in her eyes as she stares at me.

I don't even blink.

My left hand grabs her by the scruff of her neck, pulling her backwards. She refuses to let go, digging her teeth further into my arm. I pause, adjust my grip, they yank her backwards, tearing her off me. She leaves with a chunk of my arm still clamped between her lips, the bloody flesh dripping onto her chest. She squirms in my grasp, trying to wriggle free, but my grip is too tight.

The others try to take advantage of my distraction, coming at me as one. A stomp kick to the knee of one of the men folds it backwards as he draws close, sending him stumbling to the floor in a moaning heap. I swing the woman around at the other four, her outstretched kicking feet level with the heads of the oncoming attackers. Two of them are sent reeling, their own blood mingling with the drying blood of their victims. The other two have the foresight to jump back, opening up the distance once again.

The woman in my left hand is still struggling. I bring her round in front of me, looking up at her furious eyes, her anger now tinged with fear. My right hand reaches forward, my fingertips touching the sides of her neck.

I am drenched in a bright arterial spray as I tear her throat out, the flesh soft and yielding as my fingers dig through it and rip it out. I drop her body as I spin into a kick, this one at the head of the man with the broken leg. His head snaps sideways with an audible crack, and he collapses, limp. The outlines of broken vertebrae protrude through the flesh of his neck.

Four left.

By this point, their rage is replaced by desperation and fear. Their movements become jerky and unsure. They're second guessing themselves, not used to being on the losing side of a fight.

One of the women swings a clumsy punch at me. I catch the fist, twist the arm into a lock, then bring the palm of my hand down on the back of her elbow. The bone splinters, sticking through the skin, as the arm inverts. Still gripping her hand, I ram the jagged end into her throat, blood streaming down her neck. A single punch of my own caves in the skull of another woman, leaving her tottering drunkenly around as her brain tries to comprehend the damage. One woman and one man remain. He turns and tries to run, leaving the woman to face me alone. Before she has a chance to prepare, I'm upon her, my fingers already plunging into her eyes, pushing through the jelly-like mass and into the sockets. She screams, her mouth stretching wide enough for me to see her tonsils.

I grab her bottom jaw with my right hand, her top with my left. Were she conscious enough to be aware of what I was doing, she could easily rob me of my fingers by clamping her teeth down. But she is in too much pain, her mind overloaded. I wrench my hands in opposite directions. Her cheeks tear themselves to pieces as I rip her head in two, a bloody smile that stretches ear to ear.

One to go.

He's banging on one of the closed doors, jabbering incoherently. He glances back over his shoulder, sees me coming, and begins screaming, pounding on the metal desperately.

It's no use.

I crush him against the door, my left hand on his shoulder, pinning him in place. I draw my right arm back, then shunt it forward, into his back. And then through it. He screams and writhes as my fist closes around his spine, the bone hard and sharp against my palm. His sound and movement abruptly stop as I pull the spine from his body, the bloody column ripping the skin of his back apart as I pull it free. His body falls limp, and I drop it to the floor.

Twenty-five people had stepped into this room.

Now, there are twenty-four corpses.

And me.

Still there? Not rushed off to throw up your lunch? Good. Yeah, sorry about that one. Not the most pleasant of reading experiences. If you know me, you're probably wondering how the hell I actually managed to write this (my squeamishness is well documented). No easy answer to that one really, other than I just sat down and wrote it. Not much more to say.

This story was something of a manifestation of some anger and frustration I was feeling at the time I wrote it, which came from a number of causes that I'm not going to get into here. I wanted some kind of outlet or way to express that, so I just decided to write a balls-to-the-wall brutal slaughter. The fight itself, and the brutal executions within it, were somewhat inspired by the glory kills in the games Doom (2016) *and* Doom: Eternal *(even though the latter wasn't actually out at the time I wrote this). I actually planned to make this a much longer story, with the unnamed protagonist fighting their way through multiple arenas of enemies. Each one would provide them with new weapons from different settings (think everything from swords to staffs, crossbows to cannons, lasers to light machineguns), and have them mercilessly killing people with them. I wanted this to be a longer project that I could keep coming back to every time I needed to blow off steam, the literary equivalent of punching a pillow, if you like. But for some reason, I just didn't. I guess I've never felt that angry about anything since (which is surprising, given some of the stuff that's happened in recent times). But then, I guess that's a good thing. If I haven't gotten that worked up about anything in the intervening time, I suppose that means things are doing somewhat better. Maybe I will come back to it at some point in the future, whether that's out of need to de-stress or just a desire to tell more of this story. But for now, at least,* Rip and Tear *will remain a single, bloody, brutal instance of me letting out my frustrations.*

Semper Fi

(Warning: Graphic Violence)

Someone once asked me, "Do you know what an artist and a sniper have in common?"

"No," I shook my head after a moment's deliberation, "tell me."

"Details." The reply came with a wry smile. "Like, when a touch of colour is out of place. When a shadow does not match with its surroundings. When a shape is not where it is supposed to be."

There was an explosive cough, followed by a soft click of metal tapping against concrete as he took his eye away from the scope. I knew, without having to look through my own scope, that the target had fallen. John Calmers never missed.

"The only difference is the stakes," he finished, smiling at me under the hot Afghani sun. "Ours are higher."

*

That day, at the makeshift range outside our base of operations in the Registan Desert, comes back to me now, as I lie beneath a different sky, holding a different rifle, to shoot a very different kind of target. No more black silhouettes on metal plates, no more friendly rings peering out of the long grass. Here, today, I will fire a real bullet into real flesh, real blood, and real bone. I will be robbing a man of his life, a mother of a son, a wife of a husband.

I will be committing the worst sin a human being can perform. I will change the world, permanently, irreversibly.

Just as I have so many times before.

*

Calmers taught me everything I needed to know about sniping. But I'd been handling guns almost since I could walk. You don't grow up on a ranch in Texas without learning a thing or two about firearms. My father was in the Marines too, as a combat medic, and as a boy I'd always loved to hear the stories he brought back with him from his tours. It was my father who first taught me how to clean, maintain, aim and fire a gun.

But it was Calmers who taught me how to shoot.

"Being a sniper," he told me, "is more than just lining up the crosshairs and pulling the trigger. It's more than just spotting a target and taking a shot. If that was all there was to it, any old fool with a rifle could be considered a sniper. It's about precision. It's about awareness. It's about control."

I nodded, eyes wide, trying to absorb everything he said. Here I was, a fresh-faced marine, out on his first tour of duty, next to a shooter so legendary that the Taliban had put a bounty of four hundred thousand US dollars on his head. He was the Vincent Van Gogh of sniping, and I was a kindergartener with wax crayons.

"Tell me, Icarus, what's the longest shot you've made where you hit your target with any degree of accuracy?"

"Nine hundred and seventy-two yards, sir," I replied instantly. It was a figure I knew by heart, and was immensely proud of. However, even as I said it, I could tell by Calmers's face that he wasn't impressed.

"What calibre?"

"Lapua Magnum .338, sir."

"Cut the 'sir' bullshit, Icarus. I ain't your superior. I'm a marine sniper, a Private First Class same as you. The only difference is experience." He paused to look me up and down. "Nine hundred and seventy-two yards, with a .338? That's good. On your daddy's range was it? Nice clear day, little wind, static metal plate target?"

I nodded.

"Would you like to know my record for a .338?"

I nodded again. Looking back, I probably should have been annoyed. I'd been so proud of that shot, and here Calmers was, seemingly belittling it. But, somehow, I knew he wasn't trying to put me down. Rather, he was trying to size me up.

"Twenty-two hundred, forty-nine yards. Give or take."

My mouth dropped open.

"Target was a Taliban driver, taking half a dozen of them from their cave to one of the local towns. Wind was kicking up a bitch of a sandstorm that they were trying to use for cover. Thought they could slip in and lay an ambush for when a convoy of our boys came through later. It was smart. Would've worked, too. But there was one thing they didn't count on: me, perched on a ridge more than a mile and a half away. I'd been there all night and all day, without moving, without sleeping. Just waiting. And then, I see them making their way through the storm. Wasn't hard to make out the RPGs they had in the back with them, and working out what they were doing." He paused, his eyes far away. "Tell me, Icarus. That shot you made with the .338. How did you feel just before you fired?"

I hesitated, unsure how to respond. "I felt like I was the only person in the world." My reply was slow, measured. "I was aware of everything. The wind, the sun, my father behind me. But I didn't care about any of it. It was just me, the target, and the gun." I shook my head. "No, it wasn't quite like that. I felt like the gun and I were one, that it was a part of me ..." I trailed off, embarrassed. But when I looked up at Calmers I saw no contempt or scorn in his eyes. Instead, he was looking at me with approval, maybe almost pride.

"That's good, Icarus. That's very good," he said after a moment. "That's the feeling that you want every time you take a shot. That detachment from reality, where nothing matters but what you're aiming at. You learn to replicate that, and that nine seventy-two shot will seem like child's play on a bad day. They sent you out here because you can
shoot, Icarus. But I'm going to teach you how to snipe."

*

The concrete of the rooftop is hard and uncomfortable beneath my elbows and chest. It matters little to me. I ceased to care about things like comfort a long time ago.

Now, I put my eye to the Schmidt & Bender 5-25x56 PM II/LP telescopic sight and examine the area where my target will arrive in just a few minutes. The scope is attached to an Accuracy International AWM L115A3 sniper rifle. This is the same model that Calmers used for his record-breaking shot at the Taliban truck driver, although his was chambered, as he said, for the .338 Lapua Magnum round. Mine is fitted for the slightly smaller .300 Winchester Magnum cartridge. The smaller bullet offers greater muzzle velocity and resistance to wind interference, at the cost of a reduced effective range. The .338 round would allow me a greater range of positions from which to take the shot, but comes with one inescapable flaw. The cartridges do not fit properly in the magazine, as the rifle was initially designed for smaller rounds, and has to be modified for use with .338. This very slightly increases the risk of the round chambering incorrectly. A minor consideration, but a risk that is not worth taking.

In this business, no risk is worth taking.

*

"What are some of the factors that a sniper, shooting at long ranges, must consider?" Calmers asked, standing beside a chalkboard in the briefing tent. This 'lesson' wasn't Calmers deciding that he needed to teach me. I'd asked him to make me a better sniper, and although, as he'd pointed out, he wasn't technically my superior, his years of experience and sheer unparalleled skill made him superior.

"Wind direction and speed." The responses were automatic, instinctive. "Elevation relative to, and distance from, the target. At extreme ranges, the Coriolis effect caused by the Earth's rotation must also be considered."

"Very good, Icarus." Calmers wrote the items on the board. "The only one you missed is air density."

"Air density?" I repeated, a little confused.

"Yes. Think back to your high school physics classes. When light is travelling through air, and then it hits the surface of the water, it bends."

"Because the water is more dense," I replied, remembering what I'd been taught. "The light slows down, but if it's travelling at an angle it bends because one side of the ray hits the water first and slows down first."

"Exactly. Now imagine that the ray of light is a bullet's flight path. The principle is exactly the same. If your bullet enters a patch of air that is significantly more or less dense than the air you fired it into, its trajectory can change. Just the tiniest amount."

"But at long ranges, that tiniest amount can be the difference between putting a bullet between someone's eyes, and shooting their ear off," I finished for him.

He nodded. "Right on. This is at the very heart of long-range shooting. Each and every one of these variables," he tapped down the list on the board, "must be accounted for. You've got to be aware of everything, every minute detail, before you take the shot." He paused to look at me. "Believe it or not, that's actually the easy part."

"I know." I'd already worked out what he was going to say next. "The hard part is blocking it all out when you take the shot."

*

The wind is blowing across the river, east to west. Looking once more through my scope, I catch sight of a paper streamer tied to a lamppost across the water, fluttering slightly in the breeze. About five or six knots, judging by the dancing strip. I momentarily wonder if anyone will ever guess its significance, its relation to this event. I adjust the settings of the scope accordingly, the wheel clicking smoothly beneath my thumb. I already know the distance from my nest to the point where my target will appear: two thousand, three hundred and fifty-six yards. Just over one hundred yards longer than the shot which Calmers had been so proud of.

*

All the stories, the legends, that I'd heard about John Calmers paled in comparison to the man himself. He was more than just a soldier, more than a sniper. He was an aficionado, an artist.

"You hear about what happened at that school?" I asked one of my squad mates, a cheerful Californian named Matthew, one day as we sat in the searing sun, cleaning and maintaining our radios.

"No?"

"There was a school out in Helman Province. They'd been running secret classes for women and girls, and, well, you know what the Taliban thinks about that." I could almost feel the twinkle in my eyes as I disassembled the radio. I loved telling this story, even though it was not my own. "Calmers and his spotter were on patrol in the area, just under a mile away, when they see a whole platoon driving up the track towards the school. They could have left it, moved on. No one would ever have known they were there.

"But they didn't." I glanced over at Matthew, unable to keep the awe and admiration from my voice and face. "He took on the entire platoon by himself. He picked them off one by one, moving from hide to hide, taking shot after shot for forty-two hours. He didn't sleep, he didn't eat. He just shot. And shot. And shot. He killed, and killed and killed. There was nothing they could do. Every time they thought they were safe, he took another one of them out. Eventually they just upped and left. They'd lost too many men."

"How many did he get?" Matthew asked, and I could hear the awe in his voice too.

"Official count stands at fifty-three." I paused, and smiled to myself. "Thirty-seven of them were headshots."

"Oh, come on." Next to me, the other man shook his head. "That's just showing off."

"Taliban won't go near that place anymore. Say it's cursed. Being honest, I can't blame them." I glanced across the open compound to where Calmers had just appeared out of the mess tent. "That man is the angel of death."

*

A sniper's bullet will kill you one of three ways, depending on where it hits.

First, the extremities. Even if it misses a major artery, the large calibre round will cause extreme blood loss. You'll bleed out in ten to twenty minutes.

Second, centre mass, anywhere in the chest. The bullet will tumble, lots of bone to splinter. Hit an artery or any of the major organs, blood pressure drops to zero.

And finally, the headshot. Middle of the skull, any angle. Like a marionette with the strings cut, you're dead before your brain can process what's happened.

All trainee snipers and marksmen are taught to go for the second option. It's a much larger target, one that tends to move slower and less frequently than the head or limbs. It can't bob or duck or flinch back. It's logical, sensible. But there's a reason snipers in movies always shoot for the head.

It's more cinematic, for a start. When a large calibre rounds meets a skull, it bores a neat little hole in the bone, cutting cleanly into the cranial cavity. The entry hole is about the size of your finger, and looks like it could have been made by a nail.

The bullet will then tunnel through the soft brain matter before exiting the skull. But this time, the hole it leaves is the size of your fist. It's as if someone has used a rock to smash open the skull from the inside. At the same time, hydrostatic shock caused by an immense pressure wave will liquify the brain tissue, and eject it through the exit hole. In some cases, this pressure wave is so great that the head will literally explode, causing an instantaneous decapitation.

A body shot is more likely to land, but a headshot is certain to kill.

I've undertaken more than four dozen contracts since I was discharged from the Marines. Every time, I have to thank my training for allowing me to make the kill.

But there is one part of it I always ignore.

I always aim for the head.

*

I should have died that day, really. Indeed, I would have, twice, were it not for Calmers.

The ridge we were lying on was rocky and uncomfortable, with loose stones sliding under my elbows and tufts of tall, dry grass scratching at my face. The sun was as merciless as ever, baking the two of us as we lay, unmoving, watching the town through our scopes.

"Cowboys One and Two, this is Cowboy Actual. What's your twenty? Over."

"Cowboy Actual, this is Cowboy One," Calmers answered through his radio mic. "Village is quiet. No traffic in or out for the last two hours. Our boy's not going anywhere. Over."

"Copy that, Cowboy One. Maintain overwatch while we extract the target. No one gets near that village. Understand? Over."

"Understood, Cowboy Actual. Go get 'em. Cowboy One over and out."

I glanced over at my partner, doing my best to keep my nerves down. Calmers was always so composed, so controlled. By contrast, my palms were sweaty, my stomach was trying to replicate the Gordian Knot, and my throat was drier than the sand I was half buried in. It wasn't my first mission alongside Calmers. Closer to my tenth. But even so, I could not escape the tension, the restlessness that gripped me each and every time. I took out a set of binoculars and scanned the area, making sure to control my breathing, slowly drawing in and slowly expelling each lungful of the dry, shimmering air. It didn't completely settle my jumping nerves, but it was a start.

"So, Bravo Squad enter the village from the west," I said, hoping that going back over the plan I already knew by heart would go the rest of the way to calming me down. "The target is in the north western quarter, in a house just off a market courtyard. They go in, secure him, then evac by helicopter from the north."

"And we're home in time for tea," Calmers grinned. "You need to chill out, Icarus. Nothing's gonna happen. This village is friendly and you gotta remember, this guy is on the run from the Taliban too. They're never gonna know we were even here."

I opened my mouth to reply, but then I noticed a shape moving on the outskirts of the village in a low crouch. Then another appeared. And another. In less than ten seconds there were half a dozen figures, all wearing loose robes and headscarves, huddled behind one of the houses.

"Calmers," I whispered urgently, pointing out the threats nearly half a mile away and handing over the binoculars. Calmers's face darkened. He snatched up the radio.

"Cowboy Actual, this is Cowboy One. We have armed hostiles approaching the target's location from the south. I repeat, multiple hostiles entering the village. It's a goddamn ambush. Over."

"Copy that, Cowboy One, good spot. Bravo Squad are turning round and heading home. Exfil from your position and get back to base. Over."

"But sir, what about the target? He's still in the village. If these guys find him, he's dead. Over."

"That's not our concern, Cowboy One. Repeat, return to base immediately. That's an order. Over."

Calmers glared over at the dark shapes in the distance, then replied through gritted teeth,

"Copy. Over and out."

I moved to get up, but Calmers held out an arm to stop me.

"Say, Bruce," he smiled at me. It was the first time he'd addressed me by my first name. As I watched, he pulled his radio out of his ear, motioning for me to do the same. "How do you fancy a little ... target practice?"

"But—"

"Screw the orders. This guy was gonna help us, and now they know it. They're gonna kill him. But first, they're gonna torture him. And they're gonna film it all. I don't wanna see that video. I can't leave a man to die that way."

I hesitated again, torn between morality and obedience.

Then, I slowly nodded, pulling my own earpiece free. Calmers smiled.

"Atta boy. You take the first shot."

I put my eye back against the scope, selecting which of the figures to target. They were almost making it too easy, the six of them crouching there, unmoving, waiting. Perfect targets. We'd measured the distance and calibrated our scopes accordingly beforehand and, for once, there was almost no breeze. Almost ideal shooting conditions. Easy.

I pressed the stock of the rifle into my shoulder as my breathing slowed, each breath drawing itself out. I could hear my own heart in my ears as it thudded out a slow, even rhythm.

Thud-thud ... thud-thud ... thud-thud.

I took one last inhale, and held it. This was the moment of truth. The moment of the kill. At that moment, I was God himself. I had ultimate power over life and death. Everything else, the heat of the sun, the rocks digging into my chest, the sound of muffled shuffling behind me, all faded away into nothing. There was just me, the man in the distance, and the crosshairs centred on his chest.

It was Calmers who realised what was happening. I was so focused on the shot, on the target whose life lay in my hands, that I never heard the second group of six men creeping up the ridge behind us. One of them must have disturbed a loose patch of sand or something, because Calmers whipped around like an angry snake, his rifle arcing through the air as he turned and fired in a single movement. I, still focused on the target, fired at the same time, our two shots overlapping and almost merging into one. But my shot, offset slightly by Calmers's sudden movement, went ever so slightly wide. The round buried itself in the wall a few inches next to my target. Concrete and plaster fragments burst into the air, some striking the crouching men. I still had no clue what was happening as I automatically racked the bolt to chamber another round. I wouldn't even have turned around if Calmers hadn't shouted,

"Ambush!"

His shot caught the approaching militant in the throat, tearing it open and nearly severing the man's head from his shoulders. An arc of crimson arterial blood curved through the air, splashing the face of the man behind him. The second Afghani yelled, stumbling back, blinded by the bright spray of gore. Instantly, Calmers was upon him, wrestling the gun from the man's grip before swinging it up, using the wooden stock to hit him, hard, under the jaw. There was a muffled scream as he bit his own tongue in half, and he tumbled to the ground. The other four froze, panicked. This wasn't part of the plan.

John Calmers, by contrast, didn't so much as pause. He reversed his grip on the gun (a Russian made AK-74 assault rifle), brought it around, and emptied the thirty-round magazine in one controlled, three second spray. The Kalashnikov's 5.45x39mm bullets tore through the four men, pulverising organs and shattering bones. They dropped like felled trees. Expended shell casings clinked on the rock. Blood stained the sand. Smoke curled in the air.

Calmers turned to look at me, as I stared, open mouthed. If he hadn't heard the first man, we'd both have been dead. We'd been inches away from being turned into colanders, and he was stood there, smiling down at me, as if nothing had happened.

"You all right, Icarus?"

I was about to affirm that I was, in fact, unhurt, when I saw a figure rising from the sand behind Calmers. The man whose rifle he'd stolen, who had accidentally muted himself, had forced himself to his feet. In his hands was another Kalashnikov, taken from one of his fallen brothers.

Until the day I die, I will never forget the sight that greeted me as I looked at him. He barely looked human. A nightmare creature sprung from Hell, dark blood drying on his face while fresh crimson poured from between his lips. His white robes were slowly dyeing themselves strawberry. But his eyes ...

His eyes were blazing. Pain, anger, grief, horror. And hatred. Unfiltered, undisguised hatred. The rifle came up, sand running off the barrel, its cold, black mouth silently screaming death.

My shot passed so close to Calmers's ear that he would later say he felt the heat on his skin. But the large 51mm NATO round passed cleanly over his shoulder, and burrowed its way between the militant's eyebrows. Half a second later, it tumbled out of the back of his head, an explosion of pink brain matter and fragments of skull bursting forth with it. The man was knocked off his feet, cartwheeling backwards onto the rocks. His rifle, unfired, clattered to the ground beside him.

Calmers spun around as the man dropped, watching as the body hit the floor. He noted the hole that now joined the man's dark eyebrows with approval.

"Nice shot."

"Thanks." I got to my feet.

"Come on. Let's get out of here."

"What about ...?" I gestured towards the village.

"Forget it," Calmers shook his head. "The whole thing must have been a trap. He knew where we would be providing cover from. They must have wanted to take us out and then Bravo Squad when they came through. That lot," he nodded in the direction of the buildings, "must have got there early. We were meant to be taken out before we saw them. After you nearly took one of their heads off, they'll be long gone by now. Come on. We'll get back to base, say we were ambushed as we were coming back, and that the contact is still working for the Taliban."

"And my shot at the guys in the village?"

"What shot?" He looked at me pointedly.

"Right. What shot," I repeated, as we started to trudge our way down the ridge.

*

I used to feel guilty about the lives I took. I used to think about the friends, the family. I might have taken only one life, but I would have changed a dozen or more others. Even when I was killing for my country, I would remember each face, would wonder whether they really deserved to die.

Now, I don't care.

Not all the people I've killed for money deserved to die. At least, not from my perspective. But my perspective doesn't matter. All that matters is that someone, somewhere, doesn't want them around anymore, and is willing to make a sizeable donation to one of my accounts if I would kindly help them with their problem.

That being said, not all of them deserved to live, either. Not that I got any sense of satisfaction or moral fulfilment from killing them. Such things ceased to be important a long time ago. Drug lords or doctors, politicians or priests, traffickers or teachers. Their identity means nothing to me. I've long since stopped caring about who I killed.

Before, I killed for the country I believed in. But that changed when I realised the country didn't care about me.

*

It was as we were trudging across the loose ground that it happened. I can still remember the moment vividly. The thin, parched shrubbery scratching at my legs. The sweat dripping from my nose. The stillness of the air, as if the whole world was holding its breath.

And, far away, almost imperceptible, a glint of sunlight.

The bullet reached me before the report of the rifle did. It tore through the front of my right thigh, shredding the muscle and severing blood vessels. The pain was indescribable. It was unbelievable. My leg buckled. Forward momentum sent me sprawling onto my face. A rock struck me above the left eye as my head hit the ground, splitting the skin and sending stars dancing across my field of vision.

"Icarus!" Calmers cried out, stumbling as he tried to reach me while taking cover from the sniper. It was fortunate that he did. As he momentarily lost balance and pitched forward, the bullet that had been meant for his head spat past him, embedding itself in a rock. "Are you hurt?" He asked urgently as he slid to a stop next to me.

"My leg ..." It was all I could manage through the pain and shock. Calmers fumbled at the pouches in his utility vest and pulled out a bandage. Doing his best to keep his head down, he wrapped it tightly around my leg, ignoring my cries of pain. The bandage began to turn red almost immediately, but it would help stop the bleeding, at least a little.

"We gotta get you outta here," he said, dragging one of my arms around his shoulder. As he did, a third shot seared its way past my ear.

"You have to go!" I shouted through my pain. "If you stay here we're both dead."

"Dammit Icarus, I'm not leaving you!"

"Go! I know where he's set up. Draw his fire, and I'll take him out."

"You're one crazy sonofabitch, Icarus."

"Just go, John!" He looked at me with something that could have been apprehension, or could have been pride.

"Don't miss." With that, he scrambled to his feet and set off at a run, ducking and weaving between rocks and small, stunted trees.

I forced myself to roll over, ignoring the pain that was blazing all up my right side. My vision was swimming, my head feeling light. Blood loss. I forced myself to focus, dragging my rifle around and resting it atop a rock. I had just one shot at this. If I missed, we were both dead.

My hands were shaking. My head spinning. The scope's crosshairs were shivering over the landscape as I tried to acquire the target. The glint I'd seen had been high up, near the top of the valley we were making our way down. I pictured the man lying prone, behind a rock to give himself cover. Somewhere without too much shrubbery to obscure his sightlines. Somewhere where the incline was steep to allow him to shoot downwards.

There. I could just make out a scarf protruding from over a rock, on a small flat plateau to my right. My scope centred on the head, but the crosshairs refused to settle, dancing around it as if they didn't dare touch this man. I forced my breathing to slow, my heart rate to drop. I willed the crosshairs to still. This was it. My one shot. My one chance to save both our lives. Do or die.

And then I heard the chink of something metal bouncing on a rock next to me.

My head snapped around, coming away from the scope as I searched for the source of the sound. A small round metal object, about the size of a baseball, was lying on the ground just a few feet from my face.

I hurled myself sideways a second before grenade exploded, shattering rock and shredding the plant life. The explosion echoed around the valley, ricocheting off the walls, drowning out my cries of pain. I'd rolled myself down the slope, underneath the level of the grenade, to put myself out of the path of the shrapnel. But I was powerless to prevent myself tumbling down the slope like a runaway pebble, bouncing off jutting rocks and steamrolling parched plants. Each roll, each jolt, sent daggers through my leg, racing down to my ankles, tearing up to my heart. The world blurred in and out of focus, colours blending as dark clouds swam in front of my eyes.

I didn't even realise I'd hit the bottom until I had to turn my head to stop inhaling dust. My head and body felt separate, disconnected. My body was anchored, tethered to the ground, while my mind was floating through the sky. It glided beneath the sun; drifted amongst the white clouds.

Clouds. Slowly darkening. Grey, slate, charcoal.

Then the black clouds rolled in, and everything was quiet.

*

I check my watch. Exactly four minutes until the target is due to arrive. He will meet with my client, there will be a brief exchange, and then he will die. A single shot, straight to the brain. He will never know what hit him. He will never know who wanted him dead, or why. He will never know who killed him.

But I will.

In the ten years since I was honourably discharged from the Marines, I've never once thought about who I killed. Before they die, they are a photograph. After, a name in a newspaper. And when I centre my crosshairs on them, I don't see a person. I see a brain, a heart, a pair of lungs. A target.

Never a person.

Until now.

It's ironic, really, that what they gave me is considered 'honourable'. There was no honour in what they did, and I was certainly not honoured. After my three tours of duty, killing more men than would be believed, even taking a bullet, all for my country, what did I receive? Nothing. A half-arsed joke of a pension, a pat on the back, and a hand walking out the door and onto the street. And that's where I stayed.

I tried. I tried so hard. If I had an option, no matter what it was, I tried it.

Nothing. Nobody gave a damn about the war in Afghanistan, or my part in it. I couldn't even get a job. I couldn't get a house. My mother had died of cancer when I was still a kid, and my father, fighting all his life with PTSD, had lost his mind, sold the family house and quietly blown his brains out in the middle of Sunday mass during my second tour. He left all his money to a veterans' support charity, and I even tried them. But there was nothing they could do to help me either.

And so there I was. No job, no money, no home. I could have followed my father's example. I wouldn't be the only one. Twenty-two US army veterans commit suicide every day. I'd just be one more on the pile.

But I didn't.

Instead, I turned to the only thing I'd ever been any good at: shooting.

I've operated alone ever since. Taking the jobs that come my way. Never asking why. Never thinking about who.

Until this man's file reached me.

And today he will die, by my hand. Needlessly. Pointlessly. Because I was betrayed by the country I loved.

*

Pain.

That was all I was aware of as I made the long, slow crawl back to consciousness. Pain, of every kind, from every part of my body. A burning, searing pain in my leg and side. A dull, aching pain in my head.

And a wrenching, straining pain in my shoulders.

That was what pulled me up out of the pit of darkness, dragged me back up to the light. My arms were locked behind my back, tendons and muscles in my shoulders and upper arms burning under the strain. My wrists were bound together. With what I couldn't tell, but whatever it was, it was too tight, the tingling in my fingers warning me that the circulation was slowly being cut off. I tried flexing my wrists, looking for any slack, but it didn't do any good. The restraints were firm and I couldn't move.

Slowly, I forced my eyes open, squinting into the sunlight. As if waiting for a signal, sound began to return at the same time, disjointed and distorted, matching the blurry, dim images my eyes were sending my brain.

A man's voice, speaking in a langue I couldn't understand. Dari, perhaps. The sentences faded in and out of audibility as my eyelids drifted between being open and closed, not allowing the eyes behind them to focus.

Everything hurt. My head, my eyes, my shoulders, my arms, legs, side and wrists. But the pain told me one simple message: I wasn't dead yet.

I forced my eyelids to remain open. The light burned my retinas, but by this point any additional pain was lost in the swirling medley that was running through my system. Straining into the light, I took in what was before me with a growing sense of recognition and horror.

The room was small, maybe fifteen feet by twenty feet. The walls were bare concrete, with splotches of dark paint dotted around seemingly at random. The floor and ceiling were similarly decorated, with a large patch of dark around the feet of the chair my ankles were tied too, as if someone knocked over a can of paint. The light filtered in through two windows in the wall to my right, two open rectangles cut into the wall, throwing two spotlights onto the floor before and behind me.

There were two men stood directly next me, one on each side, vague shapes in the corners of my eyes. Turning my head to the side took an incredible effort, but I forced myself to look at the man on my left. The first thing to come into focus was the assault rifle that was on a level with my head. Another AK-74. The man's face was covered by a scarf, his eyes fixed dead ahead, not looking at me. I followed his gaze, and saw something set up in front of me, something I hadn't seen before.

A small tripod. And on top of it, a video camera.

That was when I realised that those dark splotches on the walls weren't paint. I knew where I was. I know what this room was used for. I knew how this ended.

The voice I heard was coming from behind me, still speaking softly. I heard footsteps coming around the side of the chair, watched in my peripherals as the man stepped around me. Something in his hand, something long and flat, caught light from the window, bouncing it into my face and making me squint again.

The man, his face similarly scarfed, stopped in front of me, a little to the right so as not to block the camera. He looked down at me as he continued to speak. I could hear the hatred in his voice, mixed with something else, something harder to identify. Something that sounded like anticipation. Excitement.

And that was when I decided.

This man was going to kill me. He was going to execute me, make an example of me, post my death all over the web for the world to see. And he was going to enjoy it.

But I wasn't going to just sit there and go along with it. I wasn't going to die in scared silence or pitiful pleading. I was going to die defiant, proud, giving my life for the country I loved.

Speaking was almost beyond me, requiring every ounce of strength I possessed to open my mouth and articulate the words.

"My name is Private First-Class Bruce Icarus." The single sentence came out as a strangled whisper. The guard on my left, hearing me, hit me in the back of the head with the wooden stock of his rifle. Pain exploded through my head, and unconsciousness beckoned me once more, trying to drag me back into its soft, painless embrace. I forced myself not to black out, clinging onto the pain that still burned in my leg.

It worked. I tried again, louder this time.

"My name is Private First-Class Bruce Icarus. I am a scout sniper in the United States Marine Corps, MOS 0317. I am proud and honoured to give my life in the service of the greatest country on Earth."

The man on my left tried to hit me again, but I was ready for it this time, ducking and leaning my head to the right so that the blow was only a glancing one to the back of my neck. I continued, talking over the man with the sword.

"My fellow marines, do not let my death deter you. Continue to fight for what you believe in, and never forget: *semper fi*."

Semper fi. 'Always faithful.' The motto of the United States Marine Corps. The motto I lived my life by.

The man with the sword finished what he was saying and stepped forward, his blade winking at me as he raised it above his head with both hands. The two militants beside me took a step back, standing in the light let in by the windows. The man before me was a black silhouette, a cut out of a figure in the glare from the sun. The sword hung in the air like a silver comma, lining up its downward path.

"God bless America," I said, looking straight at the camera. The blade was poised, the man ready to bring it down on my neck in a single diagonal swing.

Head and shoulders were separated in an instant, metal cutting through the tissue and bone with ease. Blood exploded into the air, splattering the walls as it had so many times before. The head tumbled forward onto the floor, blood spreading rapidly from the severed stump.

And the bullet that did it buried itself in the wall on the left side of the room. Half a second later, the sonic boom of the rifle's report echoed through the room.

The two men behind me froze, unable to process what had happened before them. The decapitated body pitched forward, bloody gurgling from the remains of its neck. The sword clattered to the floor, the blade lying in the blood of its wielder.

Before either of the other two militants could move, the exceedingly large fifty calibre BMG round, launched at eight hundred and fifty-three metres per second from the barrel of the M107 sniper rifle, ploughed straight through the skull and brains of the man to my right, fireworked out the other side of his temple, and forced its way into the side of the second man's head, disappearing from sight just as the first flying fragments of skull and brain matter reached the man on my left. Both of them dropped like sacks of rocks. Blood misted in the air. Bone chips settled on my shoulders and neck.

It was Calmers, of course. Barely five minutes later he came bursting through the door, pistol out in front of him, scanning the room for targets before the door had even had time to hit the wall.

"Icarus. Thank God." He rushed over to me, holstering his pistol and drawing a knife to cut my restraints.

"You should have left me," I managed to get out as he freed my wrists and ankles. He looked over at me as if he thought I was joking.

"Icarus, we're marines. We're more than just comrades, more than friends. We're family. We look after our own, look after each other. That's what our motto is all about. Not loyalty to our country or to our commanders. To each other. *Semper fi*, Icarus. *Semper fi*."

*

Semper fi. Always faithful.

How very hollow and empty those words seem to me now, as I lie on this rooftop, waiting to kill a man who, for the first time, I don't want to kill.

A black SUV pulls into the parking lot across the river, a man in a charcoal suit and tie stepping out as it stops. Dark sunglasses cover his eyes. My client. He's here early, which is smart. Gives him a chance to identify any ambushes, check for bugs or traps. Not that my target will have set up anything of the sort. He's a good man, an honest man. A loyal, faithful man.

That's not what troubles me.

What troubles me is who he is.

His name is John Calmers.

He's here.

A silver Mercedes glides into the lot, dark-tinted window reflecting the sun. There would be no point taking a shot at him now. The Mercedes is a custom-made vehicle, with reinforced stainless-steel plating and bulletproof glass. It might as well be a tank. Shooting now would just alert him, making him realise this is a trap, cause him to flee to safety.

I have to force myself not to pull the trigger.

The Mercedes stops, and Calmers gets out. He's aged well, not a trace of silver in his dark hair. Not that I can see from here, anyway. Looking at him, I feel a twinge of pain in my right thigh. My old wound, reminding me of the past that ties me to this man.

Calmers is relaxed and cautious at the same time, just as he was trained to be. He left the Marines some years ago for a job with Homeland Security. He'd done well there, going by his file. Something quite high up now. I have no doubt that my client lured him here with promises of information, perhaps in relation to some sort of threat that does not, in fact, exist. Calmers will probably have brought some form of payment with him.

But he has no idea of the real price he will have to pay.

It's funny. I thought I'd cast out every last shred of humanity I'd ever had. No family, no friends, no faith, no compassion, cares or connections. Just a triggerman, a killer, a ghost.

But, as I lie here, my heart rate gradually slowing in preparation for the shot I don't want to take, I realise something. Years of killing whoever, wherever, whenever for whatever reason, is not quite enough to completely destroy a man's soul. It's not enough to make me kill my comrade.

I force all these thoughts from my mind, pressing my eye to my scope. Who he is or was doesn't matter. All that matters is what he shortly will be: nobody. A dead man. A headline, read and then forgotten and swept away.

Calmers and my client are talking, likely ensuring neither of them were followed. I make myself stop seeing a fellow soldier where Calmers stands. He's just a target, a series of vital zones connected by a complicated network of vessels.

My breathing slows, my heart rate drops. The crosshairs centre on the head of my mentor – target. Everything else falls away. The hard concrete beneath my elbows and chest. The wind brushing through my hair. The muffled shuffling from behind me. It is just me, the crosshairs, and my friend.

No.

I spin over onto my back, dropping my rifle and drawing my handgun (a suppressed FN Five-seveN semi-automatic pistol) in the same movement. The safety is off, a round already chambered, and I snap off two shots in quick succession; the 5.7x28mm bullets catching the man behind me in the chest. The thick Gemtech SFN-57 suppressor reduces the sound of the shots to two angry cracks. The man stumbles backwards towards his friends, his own pistol falling to the floor with a clatter. The first of his comrades snaps up his gun, a .22 calibre Ruger pistol, equipped with a silencer similar to my own, aiming for my heart.

I scissor his load-bearing leg between both of mine, bending my knees sharply to pull his leg out from under him. His other comrade takes another double tap from me, one to the chest, one to the head, before the man's head can even smack down on the tarmac. I release his leg, roll over again, and put a fifth shot between his eyes. The expended brass case clinks on the concrete. Blood pools around the bodies.

There had been three men attempting to ambush me. In the space of only twice as many seconds, they had become three corpses.

I crawl back over to the rifle, slipping the pistol back into its holster as I go. I pull the stock into my shoulder, pressing my eye once more against the scope. It's not hard to work out what's just happened. Perhaps I should even have expected it, knowing the kind of person I was dealing with. But I'd been thrown right from the start, by seeing Calmers's name on the file. Maybe it caused me to be careless. Maybe it made me make mistakes.

Well, that won't matter now. It's time to finish what I started when I accepted this contract.

The two men are still standing in the parking lot, talking, maybe rehashing their agreement. Once more, my heart dips in its rhythm. My breathing slows. The black cross settles on the head of my target, who's smiling, as if pleased with what he's hearing.

Next to him, Calmers smiles back.

Pink mist swirls in the air, as brains dance across the tarmac.

Semper Fi

Another graphic one, sorry. But hey, at least this one wasn't just about brutal violence. That was just a part of the story. A lot of people don't seem to realise just how much damage a sniper's bullet will do. I mean these are chunks of metal, nearly a centimetre across, travelling at speeds of over three and a half thousand kilometres per hour. If one of those hits you, it's not going to be pretty. And that's what I really wanted to convey here. Sniping is often considered something of a detached way of killing your enemies, almost a cowardly act. I feel a lot of people would be more comfortable killing someone if they could do it from over a kilometre away without having to look directly at what they've done. Well, I wanted the reader to see what it was like. I wanted it to be brutal, visceral, something they couldn't ignore. At the same time, I didn't want all that to just be thrown at them in one go. That's why I made the central character something of a learner. I wanted the reader to learn along with Icarus, let them discover the realities of sniping as he did.

I'll give credit where credit's due; part of my inspiration, and a major influence on this story, was the Netflix series Shooter, staring Ryan Phillippe. I still say that the first season of that show is one of my favourite shows ever. I know it's not great if you look at it from a critical standpoint, but damn do I enjoy it. Like Semper Fi, it wasn't afraid to show the brutal reality of sniping, and I liked that. Since writing this, I actually adapted Semper Fi into screenplay format for one of my university modules (and got a first for it, which was a pleasant surprise). I would definitely put this story among my favourites that I've written. There are a couple of things I'd change (the names of the characters, for one), and I know that the depiction of war, and particularly the opposition the marines are facing, is shallow and a *little outdated. But despite that, I still love this story. It was a pleasure for me to write, and I hope you enjoyed reading it as much as I did.*

The Diary

A pothole in the road smacks my head painfully into the metal above me, sending stars and sparks dancing before my eyes. A faint warm trickle, almost lost in the sweat that coats my scalp, runs between the roots of my hair and slides under my collar. As I thump back down against the floor, the low rumble of the engine fills my ears, driving the wheels over the uneven road.

I don't know where I am, and I don't know who they are.

But I know one thing.

They're going to kill me.

They snatched me as I was coming out of the office, in broad daylight no less. Grabbed me and threw me into this car, a brown Ford Cortina. There are three of them. I didn't hear any names, but mentally I've assigned them some based on appearance. The one who threatened me with a gun, huge and brutish, but surprisingly well spoken; he's The Interrogator. The small, round man, who seemed almost nervous being present, I think of as Mr Toad, although why the eccentric aristocrat from *The Wind in the Willows* was the first thing to come to mind is beyond me.

And then there's him.

The leader.

The one who watched from the corner, his confident, cocky grin revealing his 12-carat dentistry.

Gold Tooth.

The car stops.

I hear footsteps getting out.

I have to do something; try and get away. They didn't tie me up before they threw me in here, God knows why. I have to surprise them, jump out and run away. I have to.

The footsteps stop.

I brace myself.

The boot opens, spilling in the night air.

My right hand shoots out, grabbing at the lapels of The Interrogator, who's taken completely by surprise. Although he must be easily double my size, he's off balance from bending down to open the boot. I yank down with all my strength, tipping him forward until his head smacks against the metal rim. I try desperately to scrabble over him, but freeze as I feel something cold and metallic press against the centre of my forehead.

"Good night, Mr. Drinkwater."

There is a final wink of moonlight on gold.

*

"Ev'ryfing ready?"

"Yes, boss."

"Where's tha tape?"

"Here."

"Play it."

The Interrogator presses a button on the side of the Dictaphone. There is a faint squeak as the wheels begin to turn, then the recording begins.

"Read this."

"Who are you? Where am I?"

"Read it." Even through the tinny speaker, the sound of a gun cocking is unmistakable.

"What're—? Who are you people?"

"Read it, Mr. Drinkwater."

A pause.

"My name is Eric Drinkwater. I'm a financial advisor. Three years ago I started tricking the elderly and vulnerable into investing money with me. I took their money with no intention of ever paying them anything back. What is this? I don't—"

"Mr. Drinkwater, don't play innocent with us. We know exactly who you are. If I have to ask you to read the card again, I will lower this gun, and shoot you through the knee." The first voice continues, now half an octave higher.

"In all, I've stolen from more than seventy innocent people through lies and deception. And now, as punishment for my crimes, I will be ... No! No! You can't do this! You can't—" The machine beeps, as the tape runs out.

"The Lord Almighty said, 'Administer true justice'," quotes The Interrogator, his breath misting in the cool air. There is a note of grim satisfaction in his voice. Blood still runs from the gash on his brow.

"Why do we always make them confess on tape beforehand?" Asks Mr Toad, a little nervously, glancing over at the car, and the body still in the boot. "Isn't it, like, evidence against us?"

"So we 'av a record," replies Gold Tooth, the one who'd pulled the trigger. "So years from now, folks'll look back at us and know what we done. Kinda like keepin' a diary or summin." His mouth cracks into a grin as he thinks for a moment. "Diary ... Yeah, I like that. Gimme the box a mo." His colleague picks up the container and hands it over. The leader opens the lid, glancing briefly at the contents as he does so. Nearly a dozen microcassette tapes, each one nestled into a slot on a series of specially constructed dividers. Every tape bears a white sticky label with a name. He ejects the tape marked *Drinkwater* from the Dictaphone, slips it into an empty slot, and peels a single label from the strip stuck inside the lid. Closing the box, he flattens the label against the lid, pulls a marker pen from his pocket, and carefully writes two words: The Diary.

"Yeah, I like it," he smiles. "'Anuva one for the diary.' Could be the fing we say after each one."

"Where are we going next, boss?" asks The Interrogator.

"Newcastle. Some guy bin doin' some very nasty fings wiv summa the local kids. I reckon it's time he 'ad a visit."

"You ever think about, you know, what we do?" asks the short man from Gold Tooth's elbow. "I know these are bad people and all, but, you know. Shouldn't we leave it to the police?"

"Police don't do nuffin', and ya know it. Don't forget about what happened wiv ya sista. Ya want folks like 'im runnin' abart free?" Mr Toad hangs his head.

"No, but still ..."

"Still what?"

"Nothing."

"Right then." Gold Tooth glances once more at his colleague, then turns. "Light it up and let's get gone." He turns, and starts to walk back along the track, hearing the lighter snap open, followed by the soft *woomph* of flame as the petrol fuse catches light. The three men make their way towards the twinkling lights of a town in the distance. Behind them, the car explodes, a fist of fire punching upwards into the darkness of the night.

Sparks dance among the stars.

The Diary

Once again, this was for a competition that gave me three things: Action-Adventure, the boot of a car, a diary. That was all I had to work with. Not exactly the easiest of constraints (how the hell do you have an adventure in the boot of a car?), but I gave it my best shot. I liked the idea of the protagonist and antagonists switching places as the story went on, changing the drivers of the car from a trio of kidnappers to a sort of vigilante group. Are they good people? That comes down to your own moral compass. But they're definitely not as uncomplicatedly bad as you think when they're introduced.

I was playing around with voice for this one as well (hence Gold Tooth's, admittedly overdone, accent). I came back and extended this story for a university piece, but, being honest, I prefer the shorter version. It feels sharper, more punchy, more compact and concise. The extended version had a brief chase scene where Drinkwater escapes the trio before getting shot. For some reason, I really focused in on the wound, tried to describe the sensation of getting shot and the pain that he went through. Like I knew anything about that kind of pain. The recorded conversation was also a little longer and more in-depth. But I felt like those bits just drew the story out, made it feel a bit bloated and over-long. So I went back to the original version, and I think that was the better call. I'll admit, the "diary" required by the competition constraints is a bit of a stretch, but I think it kinda works. Sorta. Maybe.

Cold Case

In 2020, the average NYPD response time for violent crimes was eight minutes. On this cold December afternoon, the first shots were fired at 4:32pm. The first call was made at 4:34pm. The first black and white cars arrived at 4:46pm; four minutes behind the average.

The alleyway was a mess. Five bodies, their wounds slowly staining the snow they lay in. One was out in the open, flat on his back. Two of them were sprawled behind a dumpster; another behind a trashcan. The final man was lying face down a few feet from where the alley turned a corner. Five more steps and they might have been safe.

Officer Arthur Cain blew into his hands and rubbed them together. A fresh dusting of snow had started. Flakes settled and melted on the yellow and black tape stretched across the mouth of the alley. Around him, the forensics crew bustled around the bodies. Fingerprints were taken. Bloodstained snow was bagged. Shell casings were plucked from their resting places in the drifts. Cain sighed. This was gonna mean a shitload of paperwork.

He crunched forward through the snow. The sun had already dipped below the horizon, taking the temperature with it.

"What're we thinking?" he asked one of the forensics. The other man shrugged, straightening up.

"Looks like a gang shootout. These guys got caught unawares, my guess."

"Yeah, no shit, Chester." Cain rubbed his hands together again, tucked them into his armpits. "Any guesses who they are?"

"No identifying marks yet, but we'll know more when we get them on the table. This is a Crip neighbourhood, so they'd be my guess for the shooters. But these guys?" He blew through his face mask. "Could be anyone."

Cain crouched down to look at the corpse. Poor guy had caught a bullet right between his eyes. The gaping hole stared up at him, swallowing the face's other features. This guy really could be anyone.

"Any leads?" Cain asked, dragging his eye away from the victim's wound.

The answer came from behind them. "Look at his fingers."

A figure stood in the mouth of the alley, a dark silhouette against the streetlights. He was leaning against the brickwork, legs crossed. A cigarette glowed in his mouth. A long trench coat flapped around his ankles in the evening chill, a brimmed hat sitting on his head. Neither of them were thick enough to offer much warmth.

Cain braced his hands on his knees and stood up. A small grunt from the effort misted in the night air. "Glad you could join us."

The dark shape straightened up, drew on his cigarette, then flicked it into the snow. The orange eye of its tip hissed once, then winked out.

"Check his fingers," he said again, stepping slowly towards Cain and Chester. He had a cultivated British accent. His voice reminded Cain of a snow drift; soft on the outside, hard in the middle, and icy all the way through. Chester glanced at the other officer, mildly confused.

"This is Detective Raymond Smith," Cain explained. Chester extended a hand that Smith didn't shake.

"Look at his hands," Smith said, for the third time. The other two men looked each other, then dropped their gaze to the corpse. Their eyes ran over his stiff fingers. Chester raised one of the hands. His gloved digits carefully held it close to his squinting eyes.

"What are we looking for?" Cain asked, looking up at the detective. Smith rolled his eyes.

"What's missing from his fingers?" An awkward pause.

"Rings?"

"What's lying next to his hand?" Smith asked, his voice taking the air of an impatient teacher. Cain and Chester looked at the object lying in the snow.

"His gun?" Cain said.

"Right. But what doesn't he have on his fingers?"

Chester realised first. "No fresh powder burns."

"Ah, got there in the end." Smith gave a thin smile. "So, what does that tell us?"

"This guy didn't fire his weapon," Chester said.

"Finally, you get there." Smith stepped forward, leaned down, and picked up the gun. Then he looked over expectantly at Cain. Cain didn't know what he was waiting for.

An awkward moment passed.

"Well?" Smith said at last.

"What?"

Smith sighed.

"Aren't you going to tell me not to tamper with the evidence?'

"What?"

"This is, after all, your crime scene."

"My—?" Cain was mystified. "This is just as much your crime scene as mine. We're both on the force."

Smith looked annoyed for a moment. "Yes, but ..." His sentence dried up even as it began. He didn't seem sure what to say.

There was another awkward pause.

Smith finally broke the silence. "That's a big hole in his head."

"Yeah, poor fucker." Chester grimaced. "No chance of an open casket for this guy."

"Actually, you're on to something there, Smith," Cain said, leaning in too. "That's a damn big hole. Be surprised if that came from a handgun." He glanced at Chester. "You dig the bullet out of this guy's skull yet?"

Chester shook his head. "No, haven't extracted any of them yet. Normally do that on the autopsy table. Why?"

"Can you get this one out now?'

"Why?"

"Just a theory."

Chester shrugged. "Sure. It'll take me a minute though." He glanced down the alley. "You guys might wanna check the other ones while I do. This ain't gonna be pretty."

Cain nodded. Together, he and Smith made their way down towards the other splayed corpses. The attending forensics stood back to let them look. The story on the other four bodies was pretty similar. Multiple gunshot wounds, the leaking blood slowly freezing. They crouched down beside the one at the end of the alley. The man's face was buried in the snow. His thin woollen beanie had stiffened with ice. He'd been wearing wool gloves too, but one had been removed. Cain assumed the forensics had done it to take fingerprints. Smith gently took hold of the man's head and lifted it. He studied the bullet wound in the back of the neck.

"Is that an entrance or an exit wound?"

Cain leaned over to get a closer look. "Too clean to be an exit. I'd say definitely entrance."

"So, he was shot in the back of the neck."

"I reckon so."

"The first body we looked at, who was shot in the head," Smith gestured, "was that an entrance wound too?"

Cain glanced back towards Chester. The forensic was poking a long pair of tweezers into the man's bullet wound. He grimaced. "I think so."

"This one is lying on his front, with an entry wound in the back of his neck. The other was lying on his back, with the entry on the front of his head."

"So, we had bullets coming from two directions. Shooters on two sides."

"I thought that went without saying." Cain looked at him slightly reproachfully. Smith pretended not to notice. "So, why were they meeting?"

"Hmm?"

"If we assume that they were from two rival organisations, they must have some reason for coming together."

"One of them could have got the drop on the other. Caught them by surprise."

"That is what you would call an ambush, isn't it?"

"How do you know it wasn't?"

Smith tutted. "We know that these four," he swept his arm across the bodies, "were on the other side to the victim back there."

"I guess so."

"As they suffered the most fatalities, and this one appears to have been shot while attempting to flee, it would be reasonable to assume that, if this was an ambush, they were the ones caught unawares, yes?"

"Yes, that's what I'm saying."

"But how do you explain the powder burns?"

"What?"

"On the first victim's fingers. There were no powder burns."

"So, he never fired his weapon."

"Precisely."

Cain looked over at the detective, trying to figure out the punchline. "What're you getting at?'

Smith sighed. "How," he said, deliberately slowly, "could a man on the aggressing side in an ambush end up dead, without firing his weapon, while facing towards the very people he is ambushing?"

Cain took a moment, ignoring the rudeness, to process this. "So, they must have met before they started shooting," he said slowly.

"Ah, finally, light dawns."

"You figured all that out, just now?"

"I'm surprised you didn't. The clues were all there."

"But why make me jump through those hoops? Why not just tell me?"

Smith looked momentarily confused. Several half words formed in his throat before being aborted. He was eventually saved by a call from Chester.

"Guys? I got the bullet out."

They turned to see him holding something in the tweezers. They left their body and crunched over to him. Smith examined it first, then glanced over at Cain. "What was your theory?"

"Do you know the calibre?" Cain asked by way of answer. "Because that hole looks like it came from a rifle round to me."

Chester shrugged.

"I'm not a ballistics expert, but that looks like a forty cal."

"Do forty calibre handguns exist?" Smith asked.

"Sure, we get quite a lot of them. Could be from a HK USP or maybe a SIG P229."

"Could a forty calibre cause that kind of wound?" Smith gestured.

"At close range? Yeah, I'd say so. It's damn big bullet." He waved it for emphasis. A drop of blood fell from the tip into the snow. One of his colleagues came over, bagged the bullet, took it away. "We'll send it to the lab, see if we can get a trace on it. Any ideas on who did this?"

Cain opened his mouth to speak, but Smith got there first.

"This victim is not part of the same group as the other four. I believe that two separate groups came together here, for an as yet unknown reason. Something went wrong, and a gunfight broke out."

"How do you know that?" asked Chester. "Maybe these boys were just in the wrong part of town, got jumped."

"Because the four dead guys are Crips," Cain answered. Smith looked over at him. "I recognised the guy we were looking at, with the hole in his neck. Just took me a while to register it. His name was Denzel Zambus, known on the streets as DZ. Crip drug runner in this part of town."

Smith nodded. "Finally, you offer something useful. These Crips wouldn't have let themselves be caught off-guard in their own neighbourhood. They knew they were coming here, and they knew these guys were coming too."

"So, how'd they all end up dead?" Chester pressed.

"Two leaders of the gangs, talking face to face in this alley. The Crip doesn't like something the other said, so blows his face off. The two groups scatter, the gunfight ensues." He gestures at the corpse at their feet. "This side were the better shooters."

Chester shook his head. "But why would they meet in the first place?"

"Finally, you ask a prudent question. Indeed, we must find out." Without another word, Smith turned and strode out of the alley. The other two men stood there, perplexed. Their gazes moved from his departing back, to the corpse on the floor, to each other.

Cain sighed. "I'd better get back to the station, see what he's got in mind. Have fun clearing this mess up."

Cain left, leaving Chester alone with the bodies. He watched the officer walk away. Then crunched his way over to the corpse behind the trashcan. Snow settled on his white suit as he knelt down.

The corpse opened its eyes.

Chester started, looking into the bloodshot circles staring out at him. Snowflakes caught on the eyelashes.

"Hel—"

The word was cut off as Chester's hands wrapped around the man's throat. Already badly wounded, it only took a few seconds to squeeze the life from him. But it was enough to make the bloodstained rifle round slip from Chester's fingers. He cursed, snatched it up, slid it into his pocket. He looked down at the corpse one last time. Then pulled out his phone and hit speed dial. The other forensics were busy with the other bodies. Nobody was paying attention to him.

"Yeah, it's me. I made the switch just like you said. The round on the way to the lab will match up to one of the Crip handguns. They'll never know he was killed by a sniper.

"Smith?" He gave a low chuckle. "I wouldn't worry about him. Fucker thinks he's in some Raymond Chandler story. I'd keep an eye on Cain though. He's not a dumb as he looks. Nearly clocked the wound was too big for a handgun.

"Yes, I'm sure. Don't snap at me like that.

"Fine, fine, I'll keep tabs on Smith too. What's the next move?

"You sure they'll buy it?

"Whatever you say. Just keep me in the loop. I don't want anything coming to bite me on the ass unexpectedly."

He hung up. His breath was freezing onto his facemask. Sighing, he bent down, took hold of the arms, and dragged the body away.

This story was written much more recently than most of the other ones in this collection. In fact, Cold Case *and* Trojan *(the next story) are my two most recent works that aren't* Sola Insula *(keep your eyes peeled for that). I wrote the two of them in tandem for two of my third-year modules.* Cold Case *was written for my* Art of Murder *module and, if you couldn't tell, was very heavily influenced by classic detective stories like* Murder on the Orient Express, LA Noir, *or* The Big Sleep. *But I didn't just want to write my own version of one of those stories. I wanted to update it, modernise it, and put a different spin on it.*

I have to say, the character of Raymond Smith is one of my favourite original characters. He's someone who so desperately wants to be the stereotypical PI of old detective stories that he deliberately adheres to the cliches of those stories, even when those around him don't. He feels like a man out of time, because that's who he wants to be. I tried to emphasise that by making him a Brit in America (hence his ignorance of firearms and ballistics), furthering his sense of otherness. I wrote this to be the first chapter of a longer story, but I feel it works fairly well as its own standalone piece. Will I go on to write that longer piece? Only time will tell ...

Trojan

The two screens, one parallel to the wall, the other positioned at an angle, provide the only light in the small bedroom. Their flickering glow dances across the walls, illuminating the various ornaments hanging upon them: a metal poster for *John Wick*; an artistic rendering of the magician Dynamo, his face composed of hundreds of words; a labelled diagram of a skull printed onto wood; and a poster for a documentary about 80's horror films. Each features a face of some description, the four different visages watching from the walls. In the half light, they all seem to be brooding, threatening.

This effect is spoiled when the door opens and the ceiling light is switched on, bathing the room in a soft yellow glow. A young man steps into the room, carrying a plate of chicken and rice in one hand, and a can of cider in the other. He's dressed comfortably, loose jogging bottoms and a synthetic jersey. A pair of glasses, thick plastic frames and blue light filtering lenses, sit on his face. He pushes the door closed with his foot, sets the plate and can down on the desk, then slips on a headset and sits down, tapping the spacebar on the keyboard to wake the computer from sleep. The monitors instantly change, the bouncing screensaver replaced by a login window. Beside the screens, the black tower that dominates the side of the desk sparks into life, a series of internal LEDs glowing red, the light illuminating the electronic organs and spilling out through the tempered glass panel that takes up one side of the computer. The lights are entirely cosmetic, and do nothing much more than make the computer less energy efficient. But damn, are they cool to look at.

The man inputs a twelve-digit password on the glowing keyboard, spanks the enter key decisively, then chews a mouthful of chicken as he waits for the computer to unlock itself, checking his phone with his free hand. His desktop quickly loads, the wallpaper a piece of concept art from the *Assassin's Creed* series. The icons for more than a dozen games are aesthetically arranged around the artwork, but he ignores them for moment. He moves the mouse across the oversized mousepad that takes up the majority of the desk. It's emblazoned with more concept art, this time from *DOOM*. He double clicks the icon marked *Shrek*, complete with an image of the eponymous ogre's head. A window pops up, asking him the level of security he would like. The man selects high, and a loading bar appears. The names of cities flicker briefly within the bar, each one there for no more than an instant. A few seconds later, a new message appears: *You are connected. Happy browsing!*

The program has nothing to do with the Dreamwork's animation of the same name. The only connection is Shrek's well-known outburst at Donkey, when he compares ogres to onions, because of their many layers. *Shrek* the program is in fact a gateway to something called TOR network. The letters stand for The Onion Router, again because of its many layers. By bouncing your original IP address and location around hundreds of different computers around the globe, TOR makes in nearly impossible for anyone to track you down. Many of the computers that are used aren't even aware of it. They're just one more link in a chain that can be thousands of links long.

With his privacy established, the man starts his browser, opens two fresh tabs, and clicks on one of the bookmarks at the top of the screen. The streaming website *Twitch.tv* loads up, windows for all sorts of different games appearing as people play for their followers. The man clicks on the tab labelled *'Rainbow Six Siege: esports'*, opening a new window. Two teams are fighting it out on a sandy desert map, the commentators (or casters, to use the official term) discussing strategy and interesting plays. They are quickly muted, and the window moved to his second monitor. He has an investment in the competitive scene of this game, and he finds it helpful to have something to glance at during slow moments. He switches to the other tab and navigates to a site titled *Fantasy Quest*. This is a popular browser game based in South Korea, with many thousands of people logging in every day. It has its own privacy and security protocols in place to protect its users, making it even harder for anyone to trace him. He signs into his account, opens his inbox, and scans the new messages that are waiting for him.

Ignoring notifications from the developers about upcoming content patches and disregarding invitations to join other players on raids, he opens a message from a user named Pus_Monkey37. The message consists of a single image: a screenshot of a cryptocurrency account, showing a recent transaction to another user's wallet. The man boots up another program, this one titled *Fight Club*, opens a new chat window, copies the address, and pastes it into a message to Pus Monkey.

It takes the other user just under five minutes to connect to the conversation. In that time, the young man checks his account to be sure the transaction was successful (it was), scans his inbox for anything else of interest (one potential), and swallows another mouthful of chicken and rice before it gets too cold (it's already approaching room temperature). When the new user icon appears, the man hits the first of his macro keys, triggering a pre-recorded series of keystrokes to type into the message bar.

I trust you read and understood the terms of service?
Trojan

Yes I did
Client

Do you accept?
Trojan

Yes
Client

State the service you require.
Trojan

I need you to find information about someone
Client
Without them finding out
Client

That is generally how this works. Who is this person?
Trojan

Her name is Raven Milhon. Shes a student at Croftmore Secondary School
Client

What information do you require?
Trojan

I need to know what she likes
Client

What she likes?
Trojan

You know her interests, hobbies
Client
The sort of things she likes doing
Client
The websites she visits, the people she talks to, the books she reads. Stuff like that
Client

Trojan smiles slightly. Another shy kid wanting the easy way into his crush's heart. It's amazing how far some people will go just to try and win someone's affection.

I can do this. But may I suggest simply talking to her?
Trojan

I have no idea what you're talking about
Client

How soon do you need the information?
Trojan

ASAP. I need it quickly
Client

A rush job will cost you more.
Trojan

Can you get it for me tonight?
Client

For a price.
Trojan

How much?
Client

£300. Plus the deposit.
Trojan

There is a significant pause. Trojan can imagine the kid sat on the other end of this conversation, weighing up his emotions against his bank account. In truth, he should be charging him even more, but he's always had a soft spot for this kind of cripplingly inept social spod. After all, it's what many people would picture if he described himself as a hacker.

Ok
Client

The information will be sent to the email associated with your FQ account. Thank you for your business.
Trojan

He closes the chat window, checks the match score on his other monitor, then opens up Google and types 'croftmore secondary school' into the search bar. It's a middle-of-the-pack school in Stamford, Lincolnshire, catering to about a thousand kids between the ages of eleven and eighteen. A quick search through its website yields what he was looking for: a photograph of Raven, stood beside an easel, paint splattered across her overalls. It's one of a series of tweets about student accomplishments; apparently Raven had won some sort of art competition. That's another useful detail, but the photo is what he was really looking for. Now that he has a name, a rough location and a picture, profiling her will be much easier.

His next website is one that, frankly, he's amazed is allowed to exist. It contains so much information on so many people, information that people put there themselves. It's a treasure trove of details and facts, all sitting right out there in the open, ready for anyone to access. The owners of it have been taken to court a couple of times, but the website persists, a fact that he is very grateful for. Trojan does have an account, but it's purely a dummy one, used only to access the site and the information it contains. The email address tied to it has been deactivated, and the profile is utterly devoid of any information. Zuckerberg himself couldn't find out who was behind it.

Facebook produces multiple results for 'raven milhon'. Going just by name, the search could have taken him hours. Even knowing that she must live in or near Stamford wouldn't have narrowed it down much. But now he knows what she looks like, he can flick past most of the results. Within minutes, he's found the one he's looking for.

Raven's profile is busy and colourful, populated with posts about her art, her friends, and her horse, Sandy. Just by scrolling through, Trojan can get a sense of the kind of person she is. She likes films, music and good food. Her mother is obviously important to her; there are numerous posts of them 'checking in' at restaurants, cinemas and other venues. She's trying to build a career in art, sharing a lot of posts about competitions, articles about well-known creatives, offering her services to anyone who needs bits doing. But these are only superficial details. Pus Monkey wants something more concrete to win her heart. He needs to look deeper.

Under the *'About'* tab, Trojan finds something he wasn't expecting: an email address. He *tut-tuts*. A lot of people have contact info on their profiles, but most of them are smart enough to set their privacy settings so that only their friends can see it. Raven has evidently forgotten this basic precaution. This will make his job a lot easier.

It astounds him that people aren't able to join the dots between what they post online and what grants other people access. Take, for example, the classic security questions for if you forget your password: *What was your mother's maiden name? What was the name of your first pet? Where did you go to school?* Trojan can answer all three of those: Vienna (her mother kept her name after she married), Charlie (another horse) and Croftmore, with information he got from her (public) Facebook account. In this case, her email security question is none of those.

What was the name of your favourite teacher?

Remembering the tweet that had given him her picture, Trojan goes back to the school's website. And indeed, the art department has its own Twitter account, with a photograph of the head of department pinned to the top. Mr Richard Arkin.

Two minutes later, Trojan is idly skimming through Raven's emails. He's not expecting to find too much of relevance in them, but they might provide a couple of additional details. He notes with interest that she's set up an OnlyFans account. If she's still at school (he checks her age on her profile: sixteen), she shouldn't be allowed on the platform, which is used mostly for sharing adult content other social medias won't allow. He guesses that she'll keep it non-explicit until she's eighteen, then strip down the clothes and jack up the price. Sadly, she's not the first creative he's come across who's gone down this path to support themselves while they try to make it big. He decides not to mention the account to his client. The kind of people who pay hackers to profile people because they want to get close to them don't tend to be the most ... level-headed of individuals.

Her inbox is filled mostly with arts-related newsletters, receipts for online purchases, and reminders for her to update her blog. Trojan notes down any websites that reoccur frequently, but there's nothing too interesting here. Her sent, spam, and deleted emails don't give much away either, but that's par for the course. The very fact that he can access her email is a huge time saver.

On Facebook, he signs out of his account, clicks *'Forgotten password*?' and enters Raven's email address. A reset email is soon delivered, and her password is now his to play with. Of course, this runs into the problem that she will also get the email saying that her password is being reset, and will be able to reverse it with the simple click of a button. But that doesn't matter. He only needs her account for a few minutes.

With a new password (Pr1vacyIsKing!) set, Trojan opens up Facebook Messenger. This is where he will learn the most about her. While some people would do well to watch what they put online, most people feel more relaxed when talking to friends, even if it's through a medium they have no control over. After the *News of the World* phone hacking scandal, there was increased scrutiny on communication providers to ensure the privacy of their users. End-to-end encryption and more robust servers were made standard across many platforms. Advanced AI programs were developed to help detect and stop bot accounts.

But none of these do any good against someone who has a password.

Trojan glances uninterestedly through Raven's recent messages. Most of them are fairly standard teenager fare: a few group chats, some regarding work, most filled with popular memes; a couple of conversations with family members; and a whole host of messages to school friends. Trojan picks through them, adding anything significant to his growing profile of Raven's interests. Before long, he's satisfied that he's collected enough information for his client to make his move.

He's about to move on when a new message catches his eye. It's from someone named Natalia Walker; the profile picture another smiling teenage girl. The preview of the message simply reads, **Do your parents kno...**

Partly out of curiosity, partly out of a growing feeling that Pus Monkey is about to be bitterly disappointed, Trojan opens the chat window.

The full message is what he expected: **Do your parents know about us?**

He sits looking at the question for a minute, thinking. There's no reason to assume that this new information invalidates his research. There's nothing to suggest that Raven is solely interested in girls. He remembers reading somewhere that there are more bisexual women in the world than there are gay women, so the numbers are on his side. There's every chance that the information he's gathered can still be used to charm young Miss Milhon.

Another message pops up from Natalia, and this one does mean that he's wasted his time: **Did you tell them about any of the other girls you've dated? Surely they've noticed by now you're not into boys lol**

Trojan sinks back into his chair, glancing from the message to his profile. On reflection, no, he hasn't totally wasted his time. He's still going to get paid. It's not his fault that Raven is gay, so the client can hardly hold him accountable. In fact, he doesn't even need to tell Pus Monkey this particular detail. Let him take the information, do with it what he will. If he fails, that's hardly Trojan's fault.

He saves the profile, attaches it to a new email, and sends it off to his client, looking over at his second monitor as he does. The match has just finished, the avatars of the winning team standing proudly beside each other. There will be at least a fifteen-minute wait before the next match of the evening, so he minimises the window and sits back.

He's glad he decided not to include any mention of the OnlyFans page. Something about his client had given him a slightly off vibe. It is entirely possible, perhaps even likely, that they are nothing but a nervous teenage boy (or girl, come to think of it. Trojan doesn't know either way); in which case, including the link would result in nothing worse than sore wrists and death grip syndrome. But there is always the possibility that they're not as young as Trojan had first thought ...

He closes the thought off in his mind. It makes no difference to him who wants the information, or what they do with it. He's a middleman; a go-between. The cyber equivalent of Morgan Freeman in *The Shawshank Redemption*; the man who knows how to get things.

Trojan had once tried to explain the reality of hacking to a friend of his. The best analogy he had come up with was inspired by his school computing teacher. "There's a difference," he had said, "between information technology, or IT, and computing. IT is working with computers; computing is making computers work. Computing builds the programs that IT uses."

Obviously, the reality is more complex than this, but it served as a good simplification for his friend. "Hacking is like that. It's about working with people, manipulating them, using technology. I don't make the programs I use; programmers do that. I just use them, with a bit of psychology, some sneaky tricks and a lot bullshit, to do what I'm paid to do." His friend hadn't looked like he fully comprehended, but he was satisfied with the explanation.

The terms 'White Hat' and 'Black Hat' have been bounced his way several times, but he doesn't really consider himself either. All right, so what he does could be considered ethically questionable, to put it mildly. But all he's really doing is invading someone's privacy. The digital equivalent of peeking through someone's bathroom window. Maybe not morally right, but certainly not evil. Just a sort of grey area. When you look at it that way, it pales in comparison to the theft or blackmail perpetrated by others in his community.

He remembers the other potential job he'd spotted in his *Fantasy Quest* inbox. He opens it up, checks the account to make sure the deposit has come in, and reopens *Fight Club*, swallowing the last of his dinner as he does so. This new client (Username |II|I|II) is much more responsive than Pus Monkey, joining the chat window less than a minute after he sends the link. Once again, he lets his macros do most of the initial talking.

I trust you read and understood the terms of service?
Trojan

They have been read and understood.
Client

Do you accept?
Trojan

We accept the terms of service.
Client

'We.' That's interesting. He has come across people that do this before, usually either individuals pretending to be big organisations to appear more powerful, or the kind of stuck-up ponce who will insist on always using the Queen's English, even on the internet. Trojan places his now empty bowl on the floor beneath his desk and continues the exchange.

State the service you require.
Trojan

We need you to locate a man for us.
Client

Locate?
Trojan

Yes. We require his address.
Client
Can you do this for us?
Client

Trojan sighs. This isn't the first time he's been asked to track someone down, but it's always a chore. The fact that someone is looking for them generally means they don't want to be found, so getting the address won't be as simple as looking up in the phonebook. Not that anyone still uses phonebooks.

It is possible. For a price.
Trojan

State your fee.
Client

The standard rate is £500, plus the deposit. But this may increase if the task requires additional time or resources.
Trojan

We accept this fee.
Client

When do you need the information by?
Trojan

At your earliest possible convenience. It is a timely matter. It must be dealt with quickly.
Client

Why is that?
Trojan

That is not your concern. Just find him.
Client

You haven't told me who I'm looking for.
Trojan

We will send you his information.
Client

You will receive your payment upon delivery of his address.
Client

The client disconnects from the chat window, with more than a hint of someone defiantly leaving a room and slamming the door. Trojan sits there for a minute, contemplating his task. Finding someone is a chore, but normally doable. He can often jack up the price as well, if for no other reason than to compensate for the tedium of it. A simple enough job.

But something feels off.

It's the little details. Things like the client's FQ username, |Il|I|Il. This is what is known as a 'barcode' username, often used by people who either lack imagination or don't want their name connected to them. It consists of varying combinations of capital 'I's, lowercase 'L's, and vertical bars, which can be found on the same key as the backslash. Most barcode names are kids trying to be edgy, usually hacking in online games. But they can be useful for providing small amounts of anonymity. Not that Trojan's ever really bothered about the identity of his clients.

Even so, there's something about this one that's tugging at the back of his mind. It's the way they answered his questions, not giving anything away, not telling him why they were looking for this person. Hell, they wouldn't give him the guy's name until the job was confirmed.

And then there's that single word.

'We.'

He shakes his head, shrugs, and leans forward. Whoever or whatever they may be is none of his concern. As long as they pay, they could be anyone from the corpse of Tom Clancy to the Queen of Sheba for all he cares.

A notification in the bottom corner of his screen tells him that he's received a new file through FQ's sharing service. He quickly scans it for viruses (always worth doing) and, upon finding it clean, opens it and begins to read.

The document is much more detailed than he'd been expecting. Beyond the guy's name (James Jeanson-Mitnick), age (27), and last known address (12 Peel Close, Charlton Kings, Cheltenham, GL53 8QH), they've also supplied his National Insurance number, his contact details, even his car's number plate. Hell, they've done half the work for him. Whoever these people are, they're well connected.

Trojan begins, as he usually does, with a social media search. The information superhighway, to give the internet its archaic original name, throws an immediate roadblock up in front of him this time. Jeanson-Mitnick (Trojan mentally abbreviates it to JM) has no social media presence. At all. Facebook, Twitter, Instagram, even TikTok and Pintrest. No accounts connected with that name that match JM's description. He shrugs to himself. A lot of people consider having no social media a personality trait these days, although Trojan's always thought it demonstrates a lack of personality.

He pulls a burner phone out of one of the draws of his desk and dials JM's provided mobile number. The phone, like his computer, is equipped with software designed to hide his location and number. He considers it unlikely that JM will answer; people tend to be hesitant about picking up calls from unknown or anonymous numbers. But you can still get some useful things from a missed call. The dialling tone can tell you which country the phone's in. If they have a personalised voicemail message, you can get a voiceprint. As long as the call connects, you can even use it to try and trace the phone's location.

None of that happens this time.

Instead, Trojan hears a polite, pre-recorded message: "Sorry. The number you have reached has been disconnected. No further information is available." The line goes dead.

Trojan looks at the phone in mild puzzlement for a moment. So, JM's phone has been disconnected. That's a little more unusual, and more than a little annoying. The tools in his hacking toolbelt are slowly being rendered ineffective. Whoever this guy is, he's doing a good job of not being found. Trojan glances down to an icon on his desktop toolbar, one he hasn't touched in a while. The icon shows, very simply, a small cartoon wardrobe, one door hanging slightly ajar. Hovering the mouse over it, the word *Narnia* appears (the name made more sense back when Theresa May was in charge). He hesitates for a moment. He's never liked using this program, because he feels it sucks all the fun out of proceedings. But his options aren't plentiful, and he's eager to be done with this case. He clicks on the wardrobe.

Some time ago, Trojan had been paid to snoop into the emails of a member of the Treasury. The man's wife had been convinced that her husband had been having an affair with his secretary and had wanted Trojan to find proof to confront him with. Trojan hadn't found any proof (it turned out the man's odd behaviour had been because he was diving deeper and deeper into internet conspiracy theories), and the wife had thanked him for saving their marriage. What he had found was an email from the man's boss containing a link and login details to a government database. As compensation for his good deed, Trojan had taken these details to use himself. That is what the program named after C.S. Lewis's tale does; it opens a backdoor into one great long list of everyone in the country.

Of course, there are probably more than a few James Jeanson-Mitnicks in the country. Searching by address could speed things up, but Trojan has something even quicker; the man's National Insurance number, entirely unique to him. He keys it in, checks to make sure he's inputted it correctly, then hits enter.

Nothing.

No results.

Growing more and more puzzled, Trojan re-enters the NI number, and when that doesn't work, searches JM's address. Both come up blank. Does this man even exist?

A quick visit to Google Maps confirms that his house is real at least. 12 Peel Close sits exactly where it should do, on the outskirts of Cheltenham. The car on the drive has its number plate blurred out. But the make and model match the description Trojan finds on *webuyanycar.com* when he puts in the number plate his client provided. So, he knows that information is accurate at least. But there's no record of JM in the government's database? No trace of him at all online? What the hell is going on?

He decides to broaden his search a little bit, just googling 'james jeanson-mitnick cheltenham'. Doing this after accessing government records feels a little bit like going from a motorbike to a kid's tricycle, but he might get lucky.

And he does.

A single article under the *'Cheltenham News'* section of *gloucestershirelive.com* provides him with the clue he's looking for. The article, dating from 2008, is simply titled: **Local Boy Astounds Codebreakers**. Trojan skim-reads it briefly, feeling disappointment rise as his gaze tracks down the page. It's nothing particularly useful; a record of how a fifteen-year-old James Jeanson-Mitnick managed to win the National Cipher Challenge (which is apparently a thing), solving the code-based puzzles in record time. Although it confirms Mitnick's existence, the article contains little of any value. Trojan's about to close it down, when a single line at the bottom catches his eye: **James also designs his own code-breaking puzzles that he posts on his Twitter. You can follow him here if you're interested in more brainteasers!**

JM's Twitter. The Twitter account that Trojan couldn't find. He clicks the link, refusing to believe it can be this easy.

It isn't.

A page comes up telling him that Twitter can't find the account he's looking for. So that's been deactivated too.

But at least he knows that the account once existed. So he knows what he can do next. He once again picks up his phone, and speed-dials a number.

Getting hold of big corporations is a lot easier than people realise, as long as you have the right number. When the call is connected, Trojan finds himself conversing with a very pleasant young woman behind the reception desk of Twitter's San Francisco headquarters. Pretending to be a member of the Cheltenham Police, he tells her that he's investigating the disappearance of one James Jeanson-Mitnick. He was hoping to find some information about the man in question from his social media profile, but the account seems to have been deactivated. Is there any way she could help?

He's very quickly passed to someone on the accounts team, who's only too happy to reactivate the account and pass him the details. He wishes Trojan good luck with his investigation, and hopes that nothing bad has happened to Mr Jeanson-Mitnick. Trojan thanks him and hangs up, using the newly acquired details to log into JM's Twitter.

He doesn't find much of use there. It's a very professional account, most of the content being retweets from people JM follows and brief updates on his life. But there is a business email address listed that immediately catches Trojan's eye. It ends *.gov.uk.* So, the missing man works, or worked, for the UK government. The sense of unease that had been sitting uncertainly in his stomach, on the fence as to whether to start gnawing, now opens its mouth and begins to chew. A government employee who doesn't show up on government records? What has he gotten himself into?

Trojan shakes his head, trying to unplug the feeling. Just focus on finding him. That's what you're paid to do. Just do it.

He opens Outlook, Microsoft's email client, and adds JM's address. He's surprised to see that JM used the same password for his email as he did his Twitter. Rookie mistake, especially for a government worker. He logs in, and waits for the server to pull down his messages.

It fails.

The address is still active, but the inbox stubbornly refuses to show him any emails. They too have all been wiped. Trojan stares at the empty page in frustration. This isn't like solving a puzzle without the box lid. This is like solving a puzzle where half the pieces are missing and most of the rest are from another picture. His speciality is manipulating and coercing people using information. How can he do that when he has no information?

He sits there for a while, turning over and then overturning plan after plan. His options are severely limited. That's the truth of it. Finally, he accepts what he has to do. It's a stupid plan, one that probably won't work. And it puts him way too close to his target. But he has no other option. He has to use himself as bait.

He quickly sets up the fake email address, being sure to make it look authentic. He has a number of pre-made phishing programs set up, ready for use. He picks out the appropriate one, generates the link, then edits it to suit his purposes. Finally, he composes the email, checks it over (removing two typos along the way), and pastes it into an official Microsoft template. Forcing his heart to beat at its regular rhythm, Trojan sends the email.

Phishing emails are the easiest way to get hacked. They can take many forms, from advertisements for products, to fake emails from banks, to messages from horny singles in your area. They give you a link, you click it, it takes you to a webpage. But it might also put a virus into your computer. The page might ask you to put in your bank details, passwords, or other personal information. It's become a major headache for companies in the modern day, as people will go to them with grievances over these fake emails.

Trojan's email has just alerted JM that an unauthorised person has attempted to access his restricted email server through a Microsoft client. He has no idea if this is a service that Microsoft actually offers, but if he doesn't know it, he doubts JM will. The email will invite him to log into his email and review the attempted breach. If he clicks the link, Trojan's custom-made program will quickly install a remote desktop service onto JM's computer, effectively granting Trojan complete control over it. From there, it will be a simple process to obtain the IP address and track down JMs location.

In theory.

For the first time in his career as a cyber sleuth, Trojan is nervous. He's exposed himself taking this route. Anyone with some knowledge of cyber security would easily spot his email as fake, trace it back to him (even with all his layers of protection, no one is completely invisible), and find out who he is. Of course, it's not the first time he's put himself out like this. It's an occupational hazard, one that's normally low risk.

But not this time.

Because Trojan's figured out who he's trying to find.

The clues were all there in front of him. He just hadn't wanted to put them together.

A government worker. With an interest in cryptography. A traceless online presence. Who lived near Cheltenham, home of the Government Communications Headquarters, GCHQ.

He's tracking down a spy.

And that begs the question: Who's trying to find JM?

A small bubble pops up in the corner of his screen, jolting him from his thoughts:

Remote Desktop Connected.

"I'm in," he breathes, momentarily wincing at the unintentional cliché.

A window appears, JM's screen floating in the middle of Trojan's monitor. Trojan watches as the mouse moves around, trying to follow the link that Trojan had sent him. The link leads nowhere, the same error message popping up again and again. Eventually, JM gives up, closing down both his email and the web browser. The mouse lies still.

Trojan gives it a few minutes to make sure that his target has left the computer, then begins to work, navigating his way around the desktop to the network settings. Quickly, he copies over the IP address, pasting it into a program that would give him JM's location. Of course, it was possible that he was using software to disguise his location, similar to Trojan. But if he wasn't expecting trouble, why would he?

While he waits, fidgeting in his chair, Trojan decides that he might as well go all the way. He quickly opens a list of devices connected to JM's computer, selects his webcam, and overrides it. An image of an office, sparsely decorated and very neat, fills his display. Sunlight crawls in through the slats of the blind behind the desk. So that rules out him being somewhere in England, where the cold November night has already drawn in.

Trojan doesn't need to speculate further, as his locator program beeps its success. An address types itself across the window, it's final line drawing all of his attention.

JM is in Fiji.

He's about to disconnect from JM's computer when there's a movement at the office door. James Jeanson-Mitnick walks into the room, talking on the phone. He paces slowly back and forth around the desk, his voice low. Trojan watches him, ignoring the voice in his head that tells him to just get out of there. He's got what he came for. He should go, send the location, and wash his hands of the whole business.

But he stays. He watches, a growing sense of foreboding filling his gut. JM sits down at the desk, his forehead resting against his hand. Trojan listens as he apologises to the person on the other end of the line, saying he can't tell them where he is, and he doesn't know when he'll see them again.

His eyes meet the camera. His voice stops.

The light.

Trojan had forgotten to disable the little 'in use' light that pops up next to the webcam.

For a long moment, he and JM stare at each other, one knowing he is being watched, but unable to see his observer. Trojan sits, frozen, looking into the face of his target.

JM opens his mouth to speak.

Trojan kills the connection.

For a moment, he doesn't move. He can still see the eyes of James Jeanson-Mitnick; feel them boring into him. Eyes that contained no anger, no surprise. Just realisation, and a tinge of sadness.

Trojan forces them out of his mind. He hunches over his keyboard, fingers rattling over the keys. He's annoyed with himself. He'd gotten attached to this job, making it more than it should have been. It was just a job. Nothing more.

He opens *Fight Club* again, pastes the address into a new message to |II|I|II, hesitates for one final moment, then sends it. The response arrives almost instantly.

Thank you. Your services have been greatly appreciated.
Client

There were some added complications along the way. The fee will be higher than initially stated.
Trojan

The 'added complications' were Trojan's restless conscience and gnawing gut, which he feels justified in seeking compensation for.

State the fee.
Client

£800. Plus the deposit.
Trojan

Very well. It shall be paid.
Client

Something is wrong. He'd just jacked up the price by sixty percent. And they're taking it in their stride. People just don't do that. Not in this business.

He clicks the *'View Profile'* button on *Fantasy Quest*'s page. It confirms what he'd already suspected: the barcode account had been set up that day, presumably only so the user could contact him. Despite every instinct warning him that he shouldn't, he tries to run a trace on the user's IP address.

It fails, almost instantly. The progress bar barely had a chance to start filling before the error message pops up.

And another message appears in the *Fight Club* chat window.

That was a mistake.
Client

Who are you?
Trojan

You should not have tried to find us.
Client

Why did you have me track down a spy? What had he done?
Trojan

You should not have gotten involved.
Client

Watch your step on the ice.
Client

They disconnect from the chat. Trojan shivers, looking out of the window.

A light dusting of snow has started to fall.

He shivers again.

They couldn't possibly ...

His defences are bulletproof.

But just in case.

He opens *Shrek* again, changes his security level to 'Very High', and sets it to rerandomise his location every few minutes. He boots up his three different antivirus softwares, ordering each of them to run a full scan of his computer. Using a custom program, he generates a string of new passwords, memorising and setting them to each of his accounts.

Then, after nearly a full hour has passed, he forces himself to calm down.

He's been doing this for a while now. This isn't the first time he'd been threatened. No one has got to him yet. If you know how to find people, you know how not to be found. And boy does Trojan know how to find people. His programs have found no malicious software, and his location is being continuously changed. He is safe.

He turns off the computer, goes to the cupboard at the back of the room, and takes out a glass tumbler and a bottle of whisky. He has several bottles on the shelf, most of them cheap. This one is a sixteen-year-old single malt he usually saves for special occasions.

Or for when he needs to calm himself down.

He pours himself a double measure and drinks half in one swallow. He grimaces at the burn in his throat, feeling it smoulder in his gut. He takes another few deep breaths, then gulps down the rest of the whisky. He momentarily feels guilty for wasting the good stuff. Then he dismisses it, setting the bottle back on the shelf. He leaves the tumbler on the dresser.

After a hot shower and a slice of plastic-wrapped cake, Trojan settles himself back into bed. The whisky is working its way into his bloodstream now, and he lets it spread through him. He's going to be fine. No one can find him.

Sleep is still a long time coming.

The next day, Trojan's phone buzzes with a notification from the BBC News app. He takes one look at the headline, immediately deletes the notification, and goes to unplug his wi-fi router to put a fresh scrambler on.

British Man Butchered in Fiji

He doesn't need to read the article to know the name of the victim. He doesn't need to see the photo of the man who he'd killed.

The next week of Trojan's life is a blur. He spends hours staring at his computer screen, refreshing and refreshing his location on an almost per minute basis. His antivirus scans are constant. He downloads and activates a fresh set of proxy servers, to the point where his usually speedy internet is sluggish and unstable. He takes the SIM cards out of all his phones, stashing them in an envelope in his drawer. Pizza boxes and Deliveroo bags pile up in his bin. His back aches from hunching over in his chair.

When nothing has happened by day eight, he starts turning off some of his new proxies. On day twelve, he puts the first of his SIM cards back in. On day seventeen, he stops running the virus scans. By day twenty-five, he's almost convinced himself that he is safe.

*

The progress bar fills to the end, the computer making an encouraging beep to indicate its completion. An address types its way across the screen, the characters forming one by one.

The man copies it into a text document, checks to make sure all the relevant details are there, then sends it to his client. The document is a profile of an individual they'd wanted him to track down. It had been a difficult job, and he could charge a pretty penny for it. The subject had not wanted to be found. But no one can be truly invisible. Not on the internet.

The man reads over the profile one last time, then closes the document, opens *Steam*, and launches his favourite shooter. The job is already fading from his mind, just one more to add to the pile:

Target Alias: Trojan
Real Name: Thomas Woodland
Age: 21
Occupation: N/A
Address: 11 Grasmere Close, Norwich, Norfolk, NR5 8LR, UK.
IP Address: 192.168.1.203

Is it egotistical to write a story that features a version as me as the central character? Probably. Especially when the story was actually my dissertation that was supposed to be kept anonymous. But hey, at the end of the day, it's my story, and I just felt like putting myself into it.

The room described at the beginning of the story? That was my room at university. The clothes Trojan was wearing? My normal attire. The details found by the rival hacker are all true to where I was living at the time (although I did change my IP address. I'm not giving you that information). Hell, his very name is extremely close to my own online persona. In short, I am Trojan. Hacking has always fascinated me, and I've dabbled in it myself over the years. Nowhere near to the extent that Trojan does, but a few bits and pieces here and there. I'm actually working my way through a course in ethical hacking at the time of writing this. One of my original career aspirations was cyber security, and hey, if writing falls through, I may end up going down that route. But I didn't want to just write about some computer whizz-kid, fingers rattling over his keyboard like it was a piano. While the technical side of it is impressive and complex, it's not the most interesting to the layperson.

So, I decided to focus on another aspect of hacking: social engineering. By showing just how much information can be gathered by someone who knows where to look, I wanted readers to reflect on what they put online, maybe even make them uncomfortable or want to go adjust their Facebook profile. That's why I tried to keep it as grounded and realistic as possible. That wasn't always possible (the Narnia program was a particular offender for this), but by and large all the information Trojan gets his hands on is the sort of thing people do put out there.

Trojan

Again, I'll credit my influences. A major one for this story was the game Cyber Manhunt, *which I really encourage anyone with even a passing interest in hacking or security to play. It's a really well put together game that illustrates the point I was trying to make, much better than I did. Even if you're not normally into video games, it's still worth looking into.*

As I said in the comments on Cold Case, Trojan *is one of my most recent pieces. If you compare it to some of my earlier stuff, I hope you can see a maturing in my writing, particularly if you look at some of my stories from my first collection. Sixteen-year-old me was very different to twenty-year-old me, who was in turn different to the twenty-two-year-old me who's writing this now. My understanding of the world has changed so much in the intervening years, as has the way I look at stories and characters. That's why I decided to make this piece, arguably the most important piece I've ever written, something much closer to home. I didn't want to write about something I knew next to nothing about. Do I think it's the best story I've ever written? Probably not. But I do feel that it's the most* 'me' *story I've put together (and not just because I'm in it). It feels like something I really connect with, a story that's really mine. That's why I decided to finish this collection with it. I hope you've enjoyed this journey through my maturation as a writer; I'm extremely grateful to you for joining me for the ride. Hopefully, this journey still has many twists, turns, highs and ... well, highs, to come. I hope to see you out there.*

Thomas

Printed in Great Britain
by Amazon